The Return

Stan Rogow Productions · Grosset & Dunlap

GROSSET & DUNLAP
Published by the Penguin Group
Penguin Group (USA) Inc., 375 Hudson Street, New York, New York 10014, U.S.A.
Penguin Group (Canada), 90 Eglinton Avenue East, Suite 700, Toronto, Ontario, Canada M4P 2Y3
(a division of Pearson Penguin Canada Inc.)
Penguin Books Ltd, 80 Strand, London WC2R 0RL, England
Penguin Ireland, 25 St Stephen's Green, Dublin 2, Ireland
(a division of Penguin Books Ltd)
Penguin Group (Australia), 250 Camberwell Road, Camberwell, Victoria 3124, Australia
(a division of Pearson Australia Group Pty Ltd)
Penguin Books India Pvt Ltd, 11 Community Centre, Panchsheel Park, New Delhi - 110 017, India
Penguin Group (NZ), Cnr Airborne and Rosedale Roads, Albany, Auckland 1310, New Zealand
(a division of Pearson New Zealand Ltd)
Penguin Books (South Africa) (Pty) Ltd, 24 Sturdee Avenue, Rosebank, Johannesburg 2196, South Africa

Penguin Books Ltd, Registered Offices:
80 Strand, London WC2R 0RL, England

Published by Grosset & Dunlap, a division of Penguin Young Readers Group, 345 Hudson Street, New York, New York 10014. GROSSET & DUNLAP is a trademark of Penguin Group (USA) Inc. Printed in the U.S.A.

Library of Congress Cataloging-in-Publication Data

Vornholt, John.
The return : a novelization / by John Vornholt.
p. cm. — (Flight 29 down ; 3)
"Adapted from the teleplays by D.J. MacHale."
"Based on the TV series created by D.J. MacHale, Stan Rogow."
ISBN 0-448-44129-2 (pbk.)
I. MacHale, D. J. II. Rogow, Stan. III. Title. IV. Series.
PZ7.V946Ret 2006
2005035403
10 9 8 7 6 5 4 3 2 1

The Return

A novelization by
John Vornholt
Adapted from the
teleplays by D.J. MacHale

Based on the
TV series created by
D.J. MacHale
Stan Rogow

Stan Rogow Productions · Grosset & Dunlap

**Many thanks to Walter Sorrells,
for his helpful insight on
this book and this series.**

ONE

Stupid! Stupid! Stupid! That's the last time I blurt out my feelings in front of a camera. And the last time I even think about a boy!

Melissa stomped through the jungle, wiping tears from her eyes and crushing all the plant and animal life that was unlucky enough to get in her way. After a moment, she got back onto a narrow path—it looked too narrow for humans—and tried to concentrate on the beauty around her. *I'm just taking a walk*, she told herself, *not running away from total humiliation and embarrassment.*

An image of Jackson flashed through her mind, and she rejected it. Just like he had rejected her. Take away the anger and the hurt, and the worst part of it was the disappointment. How could Taylor sink that low? Melissa wanted to run off to some other part of this stupid island and become a hermit. But that would be admitting she was a coward!

Best to keep walking . . . to clear my head. To get away from them all. Beautiful day, huh? I'm on an adventure.

After a while, Melissa's forced march through the jungle helped her burn off some of the anger. The others were innocent bystanders . . . except for Taylor and Eric, who couldn't be forgiven so easily. Taylor had broadcast Melissa's deepest thoughts for the whole world to hear. For now, the whole world was seven confused kids lost on a tropical island. That was the worst part, because everything was magnified—bigger than life. Wilder, scarier.

From the burn in her thighs and calves, Melissa realized that she had been hiking uphill for some time. She thought about turning back, but she didn't want to see any of them. Yet. Besides, the thick foliage had given way to low ferns and grasses, and the views ahead of her were incredible. Lush green canyons and jagged mountains with silver waterfalls beckoned her to take a closer look.

I bet no one has ever been here before. Why doesn't somebody build a resort on this island, where we can all go and be pampered? I don't think there's a prettier place on earth. Maybe that's the whole point—if people were here, it wouldn't be so pretty.

Feeling calm at last, Melissa wandered toward

the incredible vista . . . a miniature, greener Grand Canyon. She had to stop when she ran out of ground, and she realized that she wasn't going any farther in this direction. Maybe it was time to turn back.

She caught her breath at the wondrous view from the highest point of a bluff, overlooking a vast canyon full of lush greenery. Shimmering waterfalls spread like ribbons through the gullies, and the ground was still damp from a recent rain. *It probably sprinkles every day at this altitude,* thought Melissa, *and it still feels damp.* She bent down to wipe the mud off her boot and could smell the yellow flowers growing in the crevices just below her.

Just incredible, Melissa thought. It was worth getting embarrassed and driven insane to see this. The more she gazed at the majestic sight, the more trivial her love life—or lack thereof—became.

We survived a crash in the Pacific Ocean, and we survived being stranded on a deserted island. We're entitled to go a little crazy! What was that quote from Robert Louis Stevenson, who wrote *Treasure Island*?

It went something like: When you're home, you want to be on an adventure. But when you're on an adventure, you just want to be home.

That's the stage we've reached, all right. But we have to be proud of ourselves for all the ways we've adapted since the crash. It's either that or perish. Melissa wondered about Captain Russell, Ian, Abby, and Jory—the ones who had gone off to look for help. Had they adapted to life on the march? Or had they done the other thing . . . perish?

We might never know.

Her thoughts turned back to Jackson, and she wanted to slap herself. Her timing had been all wrong. Jackson had had a lot to deal with since they elected him leader, and he didn't need to add romance to the list. Being alive, being healthy—that should have been enough under these conditions.

Suddenly, Melissa wanted to celebrate being alive, even if she was alone and far from camp. *But I'm not all alone*, she mused, *not with this unspoiled view in front of me . . . and the birds and the flowers.* Melissa pulled off her jacket and stripped down to her shirt, then she lifted her arms to the heavens and stretched. The breeze on that peak felt wonderful and so cleansing.

Squish! Slurp! While she was busy celebrating, Melissa's heels slipped in the mud, and she fell backward. *"Ulp!"* she blurted as she landed on her rump. When her legs began to slide off the bluff, panic gripped Melissa. She clawed at the ground and came up with . . . blades of grass . . . mud . . . a broken root! Everything crumbled away in her hands, just like the edge of the cliff crumbled beneath her twisting body.

She writhed and screamed, but gravity had her in its clutches, dragging her down . . . down . . . down. Like a kid on a waterslide, Melissa flew off the edge into open space! She twisted onto her stomach and lunged at a rock, but it broke off in her bloody hand. Hope was gone. The vast canyon yawned beneath her feet, and Melissa could do nothing to stop her fall.

Then she crashed back to earth. Rocks bruised her, dirt filled her mouth and nose, but Melissa never stopped clawing to get a handhold. Her feet hit something solid before her hands did, and she slumped against the edge of the cliff. Panting for breath, she curled into a shivering ball, waiting to see what would happen next. Death was still tugging at her sleeve.

Finally, she realized she wasn't going to fall any farther. At least not right away. So Melissa pried her eyes open long enough to take a trembling look around. Holding her breath, she stole a glance downward and discovered that she was stuck on a narrow ledge some twenty or thirty feet below the bluff. She was bruised and bleeding but still in one piece. One very endangered piece.

Cautiously, Melissa peered over the edge to discover that it was still a long way to the bottom, with lots of bushes and rocks along the way. For sure, if she had missed this ledge, death was the next stop. The churning in her stomach would not go away, and she almost felt like puking. At least all these panicked reactions told her she was still breathing. Still had a chance.

That was, until she looked around again and realized how much trouble she was in. Cut off from people who were themselves cut off. "Oh, man," she muttered. "Help!"

Surprise! No answer came. There was no one

around to hear her, except for maybe a few exotic birds cruising the canyon's warm air currents. Her bruises, cuts, and aches began to assert themselves, reminding her of all the bounces she had taken on the way down. She had survived the fall, but that was the least of her worries. Dehydration, cold, exposure, hunger. There was a lot to keeping a human being alive, and she had none of it.

"Help!" she cried again.

Yeah, right. Help. Melissa didn't even know how far she had walked, or in what direction she had gone. Nobody knew. The others probably thought she wanted to be left alone, so they wouldn't come looking for her until much later. Even then, there was no guarantee they would find her.

Out of sight, out of mind.

This wasn't the first time that death seemed like part of the crew. There was the airplane crash itself. That was a doozy. Nathan had almost killed himself trying to climb that palm tree. Eric had almost died from anaphylactic shock due to eating oysters. Amid all the eye candy on this island, it was easy to forget that death was a big part of the scenery.

"Help!" Melissa yelled again, much louder than before. The breeze gently shushed her, as if to say there was no point in yelling. The vast canyon would swallow every noise she could make. Overhead, a bird hooted, and it seemed to be laughing at her plight.

I'm stuck down here, Melissa decided. *I need a miracle.*

Only yesterday, a miracle seemed close at hand. After more than a week of struggle, the survivors finally had enough food, water, and shelter to really survive. The previous night, they had launched a raft with a big SOS sign on it. That was their "message in a bottle" to the outside world. Thanks to Lex, they'd even had some fun racing through his crazy obstacle course.

The band of survivors had begun to respect one another, Melissa thought. They didn't take every failure or mistake personally. Where one of them lacked skills and smarts, another one had it. They were on a deserted island, but they were living in one another's pockets. More dependent on each other than they ever thought they could be.

That was yesterday, Melissa thought. *Today has been a different animal.*

It all started when Melissa woke up wearing one of Taylor's tops, which she had grabbed in the middle of the night from the floor of the girls' tent. She didn't realize it was Taylor's button-down lime shirt until morning. By then, it was too late. By then, she had gotten it dirty. *First mistake.*

No problem, Melissa thought. *I'll just wash it and dry it before Taylor gets up. She always sleeps as late as possible.* Since the sun hadn't risen yet, she couldn't hang it on the line to dry, so she hung it over the fire.

Second mistake, Melissa thought. *And that was the big one.* The fire singed the shirttails of Taylor's precious little top, so there wasn't anything to do but tell Taylor what had happened. *Third mistake.*

Taylor flipped. "I can't believe you did this! What were you thinking? This is *my* top!"

"I'm sorry, I'm sorry, I'm sorry," Melissa said a dozen times, but it had no impact on the preppy cheerleader.

"I have to talk to Jackson about this!" Taylor declared as she stomped down the beach in search of their leader.

Not Jackson, Melissa thought. *No need to bother him with a wardrobe malfunction.* She wanted Jackson to think of her as being calm and competent, someone he could count on in an emergency. She didn't want to look like a troublemaker. Like Taylor or Eric.

"I'm sorry!" Melissa claimed as she chased Taylor down the beach. "I don't know what else to say."

"Sorry?" Taylor waved the offending green shirt at her, but she never slowed down in her march toward Jackson. "That doesn't come close to covering it."

Melissa stumbled in some deep sand as she tried to catch up with Taylor. How had this girl lost so badly in Lex's maze race? Taylor could move fast when she wanted to. In the distance, Jackson was building something with rocks in a pit, and Melissa began to panic.

"Do we have to bother Jackson?" she asked.

Taylor held up the shirt like a bloody trophy from battle. "This was a gift from my daddy. Do you know how much it cost?"

"No," Melissa admitted, biting her lip.

"Well, neither do I," Taylor said with a frown, "but I'm sure it was more than your entire pathetic wardrobe!"

"Please don't make a big thing out of it."

"I'm just getting started." Taylor set her jaw and made straight for Jackson, who finally looked up from his mysterious labor.

Instantly, Taylor was all sweetness and light as she flirted with him. "Jackson, hi. I've got a teensy problem. It seems Melissa here borrowed my favorite top without permission, and then—"

"I put it on by mistake," Melissa cut in. "It was dark. But then I got a smudge on it and I knew Taylor would freak, so I washed it and tried to dry it fast over the fire and . . ."

Taylor held up the shirt to show the results. *Only the tails are burned,* Melissa thought. *The rest of it is still usable . . . on a deserted island. After all, it was a mistake.*

"Ruined," Taylor moaned. "It's not like I have an endless supply of clothes here, like at home."

Both girls stared at Jackson, who sighed with exasperation. "So what do you want me to do?"

Taylor scowled and said, "Punish her."

"What?" Jackson asked. Melissa just stared in shock at the petite blond girl.

"Melissa should do all my chores from now on," Taylor said, "and give me the choice of any *three* of her shirts."

"Three?" Melissa complained. "I've only got four!"

Taylor crossed her arms and looked unsympathetic. "It's about value, not quantity."

Melissa shook her head and tried to keep her mouth shut, because arguing with Taylor was pointless. So was stooping to her level of outrage.

To Melissa's relief, Jackson said, "Lighten up, it was an accident." He turned to Melissa and added, "Just be more careful."

"No problem. Never again," she agreed. Melissa gave Taylor a conciliatory smile and hoped this would be the end of it.

"Problem solved," Jackson said, wiping the sand off his hands.

But Taylor was not satisfied, and her stare bored into Jackson, then shifted back to Melissa. "This isn't over," she declared through clenched teeth. She swiveled on her heel and marched away, clutching the singed top in her fist.

Melissa sighed, because she believed it when Taylor made threats. *I'll have to figure out some kind of peace offering.* She smiled sheepishly at Jackson, sorry for getting him mixed up in her mess-up. Though it was really Taylor who had dragged him in.

The big guy just went back to work, piling his rocks and ignoring her. Quietly, Melissa slipped away.

TWO

Daley tied back her mane of curly red hair and watched her little brother scramble up the wing of the wrecked DeHavilland Heron airplane. Lex stopped to strip and splice wires on a new antenna he had just rigged atop the fuselage. He was trying to tune in ships at sea, maybe even contact them.

A week ago, Daley would have been horrified at the thought of Lex climbing on an airplane wing. Now the dented wreck was both his home and his workbench.

On this island, all of them were doing things they had never dreamed of doing before. Some with success, some not. Like the way they had spun their wheels trying to find food, only to overlook the seaweed and oysters all around them. Or when Nathan had blasted the signal kite and wasted a flare, forcing them to launch a sturdy signal raft.

The seven usually stuck to every task until they accomplished something of value. They could be justly proud of their survival under some tough circumstances. Near fistfights, flesh-eating rashes, and collecting food, water, and firewood were common hassles. Every day brought its share of unexpected challenges, too.

With these thoughts in mind, Daley turned on the video camera and began her diary.

Daley

It's been a week since the crash. Where are the search planes? How far off course did we get? Lex is trying to hook up the radio from the plane. He's such a smart guy, and I'm so proud of him. But even if the radio works, without a plane or a ship around, all he's gonna get is static.

Daley looked at the trees and saw Nathan striding into the jungle. He was going to forage for fruit, which was always an adventure with Nathan, who preferred action before thinking. Daley figured she had better wrap up her video diary and go help him.

But we're okay, so far. The survival instinct is pretty strong, obviously, or we wouldn't be around. But it makes me wonder how far any of us are willing to go . . . if rescue doesn't come soon and things get really bad.

With that cheery thought, Daley turned off the video camera and jumped to her feet. She didn't know why she had a feeling of dread . . . as if something were about to go wrong. Like they were about to be tested. Daley snorted a laugh.

How could we be tested any worse than this?

Nathan always left camp brimming with optimism, thinking he was going to collect a ton of food. Discover gold, find a highway—something useful. He whistled as he strode through one of their favorite foraging spots, a grove where there was usually fallen fruit. Not today. Maybe Daley and Lex had already been here, but the goods were gone. The produce high in the trees didn't even look that appetizing.

He walked over to the next stand of fruit trees, but they were also picked clean. Even the bitter little berries. *Well, no surprise. Easy pickings are getting harder to find close to camp. Just have to walk a little farther.*

What we need is a good storm to shake down some of this fruit. Yeah, but a storm like that would probably blow away our tents and wash out the fire pit. Everything on this crazy island is a trade-off. Look at my position.

Nathan had been top dog back in high school, but on this island, he was reduced to taking orders and picking up half-rotten fruit. It wasn't really his choice, but he now understood why the others had elected Jackson their leader. The big kid hardly ever opened his mouth, so he never said anything too stupid.

Of course, now Jackson was besieged every time Taylor broke a fingernail or Eric tried to cut his work assignment. He not only had *his* problems to deal with, he had all of theirs, too. That was a trade-off that Nathan was glad he didn't have to make.

As he walked, the bushy-haired teen scanned the trees, bushes, and ground, but there was no fruit anywhere. Nathan decided to pick up firewood instead, so his trip wouldn't be a total loss.

Bending down, he noticed some odd tracks in the mud and a pile of animal dung that he hadn't seen before. He bolted upright and looked around, weird primal instincts taking over his senses. All the fallen fruit gone. The tracks. Maybe they weren't alone in this part of the forest.

Nathan stopped to listen to every sound in the trees. Birdcalls, the gentle breeze, the distant lapping of the surf—they were all part of his senses now. Anything different stood out, such as those rustling and grunting sounds he heard so clearly. Nathan backed up, wishing he had a weapon of some sort. He still didn't know if he would be in attack mode or defensive mode. Eat or be eaten. Kill or be killed.

Nathan turned to his left to see the broad leaves of a fern shaking. Taking a gulp of courage, he set down the firewood and moved in for a closer look. The sounds grew louder, as if some beast were rooting around in the soil, and he cautiously parted the leaves and looked down.

A small black pig was digging for roots, and Nathan wondered what he should do. That squealer would be great eating for many meals, but it was still a wild animal. Hard to catch, and it might attack him. Plus, he would have to slit its throat or bash it with a rock. Or something along those lines. *Am I up for that?*

Nathan never liked hunting before, but this wasn't a sport. This was survival.

Something big rustled in the bushes right behind him, and Nathan whirled around, certain he was going to meet Papa Pig with his giant tusks. Instead, he saw Daley, gazing curiously at him.

"What are you looking at?" she asked.

Nathan let out his breath and gestured for her to come see. He parted the leaves and gave her a good look at the baby pig.

"Lunch," he whispered with a grin.

"Help!" shouted Melissa at the top of her lungs.

An exotic green bird hooted back as it flew overhead, and the sun winked at her from behind a cloud. The lush canyon felt like a tree-lined trap, and the vast spaces hemmed her in like prison walls. She couldn't appreciate nature when nature was trying to imprison her. Even kill her.

Melissa looked at the ragged bluff above her. She had tried to climb up the cliff wall, but it was harrowing to even go a few feet. In places, her ledge was crumbling, and only a hollow spot against the rock gave her any feeling of protection.

They've got to find me. They've got to.

While she waited and yelled, Melissa kept reliving the terrible events of the day. In truth, her problems had started three days ago, when she had been stupid enough to make a video diary in which she had talked about Jackson. Those tapes were supposed to be secret and private, but Eric had eavesdropped while she was recording.

That rat must have told Taylor. He showed her my tape!

The fact that they had invaded her privacy was more infuriating than what they had found. Heck, it didn't even seem to surprise anyone that she liked Jackson. Nobody cared, least of all Jackson. Keeping a secret . . . that's what made her vulnerable to their rotten tactics.

Her own embarrassment had left her stranded on a cliff in the middle of Nowhere Island.

As far as Eric was concerned, this island was a blast! Full of possibilities. He remembered that morning very well. Before it all came down on his head. He was just having a bit of fun. Sharing a little juicy gossip with a friend. How did he know it would turn into a big whoop?

Then why do I feel so lousy?

Taylor was testy, and all I did was haul her into the woods and show her a tape. She took it from there. I just pressed the play button and held the camera at an angle where she could see the LCD. Why should I feel guilty for anything that happened next?

He remembered the words on that tape. Neither he nor Taylor said a word while Melissa poured out her heart.

Melissa

Jackson hasn't been at school long, so nobody really knows him. But he seems, I don't know, troubled. He's gotta open up someday, and when he does, I hope it's with me. I guess it's obvious I care for him, but I'd *never* tell him. No way. That would make things too weird. But when we get off this island, I'm going to let him know how I feel and hope he doesn't laugh.

Taylor turned off the tape and shook her head with amazement. "Why, that little sneak! She acts all innocent, but then she's got a crush on the bad boy!" Taylor chuckled with delight.

Eric cringed, feeling a slight pang of guilt. Or maybe it was his upset stomach. He was still weirded out from almost dying, and he hadn't been eating like his usual self. Even in his weakened state, he wanted to make Taylor like him, but maybe this hadn't been such a good idea. The tapes were supposed to be secret.

Mostly, he didn't like the look in Taylor's icy blue eyes. "This feels weird," Eric said, turning the camera off.

"Totally," Taylor agreed. "It's like . . . twisted."

"No, I mean, I'm feeling bad about showing you this," Eric said, looking glum. "Melissa saved my life with that allergy shot."

Of course, she had also bossed him around when he was her water boy. And why should Jackson get all the girls? *I'm funny and glib, but the only guy with any chance at a babe is Jackson? The monosyllabic mystery man? I'd like to see his tape . . . I wonder what his secret is.*

Taylor snatched the camera out of his hands and laughed. "Get over it. This is ammunition—you don't throw away ammunition."

Eric gulped, because he had told Taylor those exact words when she was trying to get even with Daley. This girl learned her lessons. *And I'm her sneaky teacher.*

Taylor ignored him as she paced, deep in thought. "But now the question is . . . how do I use it?"

THREE

Nathan and Daley tracked the wild pig while it went about its rounds, foraging for food. The porker was more successful than they were, thought Nathan, because it found roots and mushrooms and other stuff they had been too cautious to eat.

It was kind of fun tracking the wild beast, while not getting too close to spook it. In truth, the pig didn't act as if it considered them much of a threat. But from the determined look on Daley's face, Nathan knew the squealer's luck was running out. It was looking more and more like the main dish on tonight's menu.

"Catching it's gonna be tough enough," Daley said breathlessly. "After that—" She made a cutting motion across her throat.

Nathan gulped and asked, "You up for that?"

"I don't know. Are you?"

"I've never killed anything," admitted Nathan, "except for fish. But that's not the same . . . except to the fish."

Daley nodded, and they took a few more steps to follow the cute black pig. They kept their distance from the animal, careful not to frighten it.

"That meat would sure solve our protein problem," Daley said.

"First let's see if we can catch it."

"Yeah. Then we'll deal." Daley shook her head and smiled. "You know, if we do this, we'll be heroes."

Nathan had to smile at that idea, because he hadn't been a hero very often on this island. It was true—in the quest for food, this would be the biggest score yet. Real hunting. Not some silly fishing or climbing a tree. Life and death. Even Jackson would have to admit that he was The Man if he could bring home the bacon.

"We'll figure out a way," he vowed.

"I'm down here!" yelled Melissa. She stopped after one yell. Even in her panic, she knew she had to keep her wits together and not blow out her voice. So she gave one yell every minute or two. The rest of the time, she just listened as she stood on the ledge . . . some twenty feet below the bluff. She hoped to hear her friends calling for her.

Jackson or Daley or Lex . . . surely someone will figure it out and come looking for me. They have to!

Her anger was fading, especially with the innocent ones such as Lex. The ten-year-old kid was helpful and accommodating to everyone. How could he tell Taylor no if she asked him to play something on the sound system? Taylor used to run the speakers before Jackson tore them apart to make fishing line out of the wires. Lex was just getting the system back together again.

How could the poor kid ever suspect that Taylor would be so mean?

Hours before, Lex was playing rock music while he finished wiring the makeshift radio antenna. The warm sun on his back and the lazy whisper of the surf were making him sleepy, but he couldn't stop working. Eric was dozing beneath him in the cabin of the plane, but that was Eric. Lex knew there was always more to do—much more—if they wanted to get rescued.

In many ways, life as a castaway was a lot more exciting than his normal life at home. But Lex knew they were one accident, one bout of disease, or one typhoon away from disaster. Look at the way Eric had almost died from eating oysters. Climbing that coconut palm, Nathan had risked his life just to scrounge dinner. The ocean was full of predators, and who knew what the jungle was full of? They had only explored a small part of it.

Cut off from civilization like they were, they couldn't afford any big mistakes. Or even little ones. *I've got to keep us focused*, thought Lex, *on getting home.*

Movement on the beach caught his eye, and he peered across the shimmering sand to see Taylor walking toward him. There was a friendly smile on her face and the video camera in her hand. He figured she was probably looking for Eric.

So it was a surprise when Taylor stopped and waved cheerfully to him. "I have been looking all over for you!" she gushed.

Lex looked around, wondering if Eric was behind him. "For me?" he asked.

She nodded and moved closer. "Yes. You are the man!"

"I am?" The boy slid down the fuselage and landed on the wing.

"You're just so modest," Taylor said. "This music thing you've got happening is so perfect! But it's time to take it a step further."

"It is?" He gulped, because sometimes Taylor creeped him out with her selfish attitude. She didn't seem to care what anyone else thought of her or her actions. That made her both scary and well-adjusted.

"Absolutely," she answered. "You may not know this, but I'm a singer."

"You are?" Well, he supposed that could have gone unnoticed in a week of living together.

She held the video camera toward him and said, "Uh-huh. And I made a tape."

"You did?" Lex asked, careful to be diplomatic. Taylor had been unusually nice to him when they launched his SOS raft. She really seemed to appreciate his efforts to get them rescued.

Taylor frowned at him. "Are you not hearing me the first time around?"

"Sorry," Lex answered. He should at least listen to her tape and find out if she was any good. Maybe a little Island Karaoke was just the thing to brighten up the dark nights. Since his successful maze race, Lex had been looking for more cheap entertainment.

"Anyway," Taylor continued with a sweet smile, "I was hoping you could figure out some clever way to hook the camera up to your awesome sound system, so I can play my tape for everybody to hear."

Lex pondered the idea, because it wouldn't be difficult to patch the audio from the camera into his newly rebuilt sound system. He had designed it for the mp3 player and the microphone, but there was probably a way. Still, he had a nagging doubt about this idea, even if Taylor was the greatest singer on the island.

"Hmmm . . . I don't know."

Taylor sniffed. "Oh, well, if it's too hard for you to figure out then . . ." Looking disappointed, she turned and walked away.

Lex jumped down to run after her. "I didn't

say that," he told her. "I'll try. Uh, is the tape any good?"

She was beaming when she handed him the camera. "It is absolutely awesome."

Lex heard a thump and he turned to see Eric listening to their conversation from the cabin of the plane. *Well, if the two of them help me a little, it shouldn't take long. Maybe it'll be good to hear some new music,* Lex thought.

He nodded and said, "Okay."

Taylor gave him a big grin and a thumbs-up.

What happened next was etched forever in Melissa's memory, and it was painful to relive the incident. It was almost more painful than her tumble off the cliff.

She had been helping Jackson gather coconut-sized rocks on the beach. Melissa didn't know why they needed the rocks, but she wasn't concerned. Jackson must have a good reason, and he would tell her when he had a chance. She did want to ask him something, but it wasn't about rocks.

What will he do if I ask him? He might clam up, walk away, and pretend it never happened. That would be the worst, and I'd have to crawl into a hole. The other possibilities are even scarier. Oh, what's the point of putting it off?

After several minutes of working closely together, she finally got the nerve to pose her question. When he bent down to plant a rock in a freshly dug hole, she asked pleasantly, "So . . . back home . . . do you have a girlfriend?"

Jackson blinked at her and looked embarrassed, and Melissa managed a pained smile. She figured he would run for his life, but he didn't try to escape. *Stupid question*, she thought immediately. *I don't want to know the answer, and he doesn't want to tell me.* Jackson cocked his head with a puzzled expression as a disembodied voice floated on the air:

"Jackson hasn't been at school long," said the amplified voice, "so nobody really knows him. But he seems, I don't know, troubled."

With horror, Melissa realized that was *her* voice blaring on the loudspeaker for everyone to hear. *My video diary!* It was like a slap in the face, and she jumped to her feet, anxious to stop it. But how? Where was it coming from? In her own words, her voice spilled her secret thoughts about Jackson. It was a nightmare happening in the bright glare of sunlight on the beach, and Melissa couldn't wake up.

Jackson gaped at her in complete shock, and she struggled to explain. But her real voice was drowned out by her amplified voice blurting all her thoughts.

"He's gotta open up someday," the speaker declared loudly, "and when he does, I hope it's with me. I guess it's obvious I care for him, but I'd *never* tell him. No way. That would make things too weird. But when we get off this island, I'm going to let him know how I feel and hope he doesn't laugh."

I've got to stop it, Melissa thought in panic. *I've got to shut it off! This can't be happening! I don't want to embarrass Jackson—he doesn't deserve this. I've got to stop it now!*

With tears streaming down her face, Melissa ran along the beach toward the sound of her voice. The airplane! As her feet pounded through the sand, her heart pumped so much blood into her head that she thought it would explode. Her anger couldn't silence her tortured words, and it did nothing to ease her agony. In a horrible rerun, her voice boomed across the sand, unleashing the secret thoughts again:

"Jackson hasn't been at school long, so nobody really knows him. But he seems, I don't know, troubled. He's gotta open up someday, and when he does, I hope it's with me."

I'm not troubled, Jackson thought. *Or am I?*

Well, he was too stupid to pick up on the fact that Melissa really liked him. He always figured she was staring at him because she worried that he would flip out any moment. Yeah, he had a temper and didn't like to promise things he couldn't deliver. Most of the time, he was just trying not to make things worse. Trying to do a little good. Not get a girlfriend.

Mel's girlfriend question had been a shock, but the voice on the loudspeaker was an earthquake. That was too real. Too much information. Now Melissa was halfway down the beach, running for the airplane, before Jackson realized that she might kill someone.

He wanted to run in the other direction, but he couldn't let this rotten prank turn any worse. Lex was the sound guy, but it was hard to imagine that the kid was behind this. No, this trick smelled like revenge. Payback.

Jackson put his head down and ran at top speed toward the airplane. He could see Melissa confronting Lex. The boy was knocking frantically on the door of the cabin, which must have been locked from inside.

"Turn it off!" shouted Lex. But the damning words continued blasting over the beach, on a cruel loop.

Melissa glared at the boy and said, "Stop it!"

"I can't," he answered. "They've got the camera." He pointed to a cabin window, where Taylor and Eric grinned at her from inside the plane. Melissa's voice continued to boom from the speaker system, and Eric held up the video camera to show that he was in charge.

"I didn't know, I swear!" insisted Lex.

Jackson reached the plane, and Melissa glanced at him with embarrassment. He wanted to say something, but it was hard to compete against her deepest thoughts blasting across the beach. Wiping tears from her cheek, Melissa ran toward the trees and ducked into the jungle. An instant later, she was out of sight.

He almost ran after her, but first he had to stop the invasion of her privacy. Jackson pounded on the cabin door so loudly that the whole plane shook. "Don't make me tear out the speaker wire and wrap it around your necks!" he yelled.

At once, the loudspeaker squealed once and went dead, leaving only the peaceful lapping of the surf and the whisper of the breeze.

FOUR

Jackson couldn't remember ever being angrier than he was at that moment. One thing they had all agreed upon was that they would keep their video diaries private, and Taylor and Eric had violated that policy. Big time. Plus, they had totally embarrassed Melissa. They had to pay for that.

Jackson didn't care what people thought of him, because people always approached him with their minds made up. But Melissa did care, and she didn't deserve this. *She's a good person, which is another reason why she should stay away from me. Someday—maybe soon—we're going to be rescued. Then Melissa, Daley, and the others will become spoiled preppies again, and I'll be lumped back with the gangstas and the misfits. She'll forget she ever knew me.*

He nearly strangled Eric when he stumbled out of the plane, laughing and clutching the video camera in his hands. "You think this is funny?" snapped Jackson, getting right in the skinny kid's face.

Eric gulped and backed away. "Uh, well, Taylor does." He quickly handed the camera to the blond girl when she stepped out of the plane.

"Thanks a lot, partner," muttered Taylor with a scowl.

"What is wrong with you?" demanded Jackson.

Taylor smiled innocently. "What? You don't think I did that on purpose, do you? I thought it was *my* tape. Imagine how surprised I was when I heard Melissa's voice."

"So surprised you didn't stop it," muttered Jackson.

"Yes! Exactly," insisted Taylor. "Poor thing. I feel bad. Did you know she liked you so much?"

Jackson shook his head with disgust and grabbed the camera from Taylor. "You would do this all because of a dumb shirt?"

He handed the camera back to Lex, wondering what he could do to knock some sense into these idiots. Feeling slighted, turning selfish and possessive, getting revenge—this endless loop of stupidity had to stop! They were acting like five-year-olds.

Lex stared at Taylor and Eric and said with disappointment, "You guys really stink." Eric looked stunned by the kid's slam, but Taylor kept smiling sweetly. All innocence.

There, it's done, Taylor thought. *Beware the revenge of Taylor when you steal my clothes and ruin them! Okay, Melissa's punishment was harsh . . . but well-deserved. And swift. My top will always have a singed tail, but she'll get over this little humiliation. Someday.*

Okay, so maybe Melissa wearing my shirt was an accident. But that's no excuse. If a cop pulls you over and says you broke a law, does he care if you did it by accident? No! Don't let Jackson freak you out—you know his caveman act. Just keep smiling sweetly.

Even though her smile looked innocent, Taylor didn't feel innocent. She felt guilty, which puzzled her. *I'm only trying to protect my stuff, which is crucial when the nearest mall is a thousand miles away. Besides, that pilot person and Ian and Jory and Abby are going to find help. We'll be rescued any day now.*

Why won't Eric look me in the eye?

Eric was backing toward the beach, hoping to escape before Jackson went after him. The big guy's fists were clenched, and his eyes looked demented. Taylor's dizzy act had him stalled for the moment, but Eric wanted to get a head start if he had to run for it.

In fact, he wanted to turn back the clock and pretend he had never shown that tape to Taylor. It was wrong that he had eavesdropped on Mel's secret diary, and he should have kept it to himself. *Why did I do it?* he asked himself.

Jackson has to be the main reason, he admitted. *Can't blame him—I'm totally into Taylor, but being her revenge buddy hasn't gotten me anywhere. Jackson does nothing but grunt a few times a day, and sensible Melissa is silly putty. I wanted to punk Jackson, not Mel. That's why I feel rotten. Even though it worked. Look at the poor guy, unsure of what to do.*

Jackson had to agree with Lex—Eric and Taylor did stink. He stared glumly in the direction that Melissa had fled. He wanted to go and find her, but he knew that *he* was the last person she wanted to see at the moment.

Now he could see all the signs of Melissa's interest in him. When it came down to it, girls just didn't know how dense boys could be. Especially when something else was occupying their attention. Mel was the nicest and hardest-working girl he had ever met, but he couldn't deal with a romance while he was still trying to learn how to catch a fish.

You can't ignore anything on this stupid island, because it will come back to haunt you. A singed shirt, missed romantic signals, and now we've got war. I should be flattered about all this, but we can't survive if we're divided.

"What do you make of that?" Nathan asked after they heard Mel's confession over the loudspeaker.

Deep in the jungle, Daley swatted at a fly on her neck and shrugged. "You didn't know that Mel liked Jackson?"

"Well, sure," answered Nathan, "but all the girls like Jackson. You voted him leader."

"Not me. I voted for myself." Daley smiled, because she was harboring a secret, too. She was beginning to find Nathan attractive, although she couldn't figure out why. Maybe it was just his energy and enthusiasm. Maybe it was a motherly protective thing—like Wendy with Peter Pan—because she was certain he was going to get hurt.

Just like me, he always votes for himself.

Daley glanced over her shoulder to make sure the wild pig was still nearby, and it was. The cute creature didn't seem to mind their company, even if they were plotting its demise. "Okay, tell me your plan."

Nathan already had a stick in hand, and he drew a diagram in the mud. "All we need is a simple cage," he explained. "It'll fall on the pig and trap it."

Daley looked at the box trap and shook her head doubtfully. The pig would have to be brain damaged to fall for that. "No way that'll work. We need some kind of snare."

"You know how to make a snare?" Nathan asked, sounding impressed.

"Well, no," she admitted, "but maybe we should try both ways."

"I like that," answered Nathan with a smile. "As long as the pig keeps cooperating."

Footsteps sounded behind them, and Daley whirled around to see Melissa come crashing through the bushes. The dark-haired girl looked as if she had a million things on her mind, and one of them had to be Jackson.

Daley grinned at Melissa and said, "Hey, Mel! Very cool."

The girl stared at her as if she were an alien with two heads, and Nathan added, "Really! We all figured you liked Jackson, but announcing it big like that took guts."

Melissa let out a horrified gasp and charged off into the jungle. Daley and Nathan looked curiously at each other, not sure what to make of her sudden departure. Daley heard the pig snort, and she knew they had to get back to work.

"Let's do something," she said grimly, "before our dinner escapes."

Melissa tried to pace on her narrow ledge, but there wasn't enough room to take more than two steps. She was done thinking about Taylor's dirty tricks and singed shirt . . . and Jackson's brooding scowl. None of that seemed very important now, when her own survival was so questionable.

After she had run into Daley and Nathan in the jungle, she had kept running until she ended up stuck in this rugged canyon. *What a lousy day this has been*, mused Melissa. *Just when I decide to go back and face those lowlifes, I almost kill myself.*

"Help me!" she shouted. Then she swallowed, worried that her voice was getting hoarse. Melissa looked up at the hazy sun, then down at the leafy floor of the canyon, noting how the shadows were shifting. For a moment, she thought she saw a person dressed in white on the other side of the chasm, but it was so distant. Maybe a sand crane. Maybe a ghost.

It has to be afternoon by now, and for sure they're going to miss me soon. That is, unless they think I'm staying away on purpose. Oh, please! Don't think that! Don't write me off as an emotional wreck. Don't forget about me.

"Help!" she yelled hoarsely. "I'm down here!" Not even the birds answered back.

Daley tried not to laugh while Nathan carefully rigged a box trap from one of their plastic coolers.

He turned the cooler upside down, lifted one end, and balanced it on a stick. Under the trap, he carefully arranged a banana on a string that was tied to the branch. Daley did her best to keep a straight face while he explained his plan.

"Pig grabs bait," Nathan said, "pulls string, yanks stick, and . . ." He pulled the branch out, and the cooler fell down. "He's ours!"

Daley winced and said, "You seriously think that will work?"

"Sure, why not?" Nathan looked hurt that she would even doubt it.

"Well," answered Daley, "because it's something Elmer Fudd would use to try and catch Bugs Bunny. And he hasn't had much luck, has he?"

"Funny," muttered Nathan. "This is reality."

"Exactly. Remember that."

Nathan scowled and lowered his head. "Okay, what do you have?"

"Plan B," she answered with a smile. "Watch and learn."

"Can we at least *try* to get the pig in the cooler?" Nathan asked.

Daley shrugged. "Sure. Let's chase him toward it—maybe we'll get lucky."

They grabbed sticks and began to stalk their prey, yelling "Piggy! Piggy! Piggy!" A chase ensued, and the porker seemed to enjoy the sport as much as the humans. The animal never ran anywhere near the upside-down cooler, although Nathan knocked it over once.

After a few minutes of pig herding, Daley and Nathan were completely exhausted, but the chase had given Daley an idea. It was a challenge now—them versus the pig. "Forget the snares and stuff," she said breathlessly. "I have something better. Do we still have the shovel?"

Looking glum, Nathan kicked over the worthless cooler. "Yeah, we have a shovel."

"Good," Daley said. "I'll keep an eye on Porky. You should get a drink of water, because you have some digging to do."

Eric had just settled down for his afternoon nap. That was different from his morning nap, because he took it in the shade of the boys' tent, not in the plane. He was getting comfortable on his beach towel, when a shadowy presence loomed over him.

"Come with me," ordered Jackson, waving his hand.

Eric squinted up at their fearless leader and tried to appear very tired. "Huh? What?"

"Melissa's been missing for hours," Jackson said. "I'm worried about her. It's time to search."

"I'd love to, chief," muttered Eric, "but I'm still wiped out after nearly dying from eating those clams."

Jackson scowled. "Look, if it weren't for Melissa, you *would* have died."

Eric sat up and asked, "What about Daley and Nathan?"

"I can't find them."

Lex ran up to their leader and said, "I'll go!"

"We need everybody," answered Jackson. He looked pointedly at Eric.

"Hey, don't lay guilt on me," Eric said. "The camera was Taylor's idea."

Hearing her name, the blond girl rounded the tent and asked cheerfully, "What was my idea?"

Jackson pointed a finger at the two of them and warned, "If something happens to Melissa, it's on *both* your heads." He stormed off, with Lex trailing behind him.

Eric shook his head, and Taylor looked curiously at him. "What happened to Melissa?"

"I guess she's still missing," he answered, lying back on his towel. "Thanks to me, you avoided a lot of searching and tromping around in the woods."

"I did?" Taylor asked with a pout. "They went to look for her?"

Eric nodded, but he didn't feel that great about his escape. Somehow he doubted if he could enjoy the rest of his nap in peace, knowing that everyone but Taylor was mad at him. Plus, she looked as if she was going to be high-maintenance for the rest of the day. For a successful act of revenge, the two of them didn't act very happy.

Tossing her blond hair, Taylor sat down on a box beside him and began to play with the tails of her green shirt. If Eric remembered correctly, that was the same top that had caused this whole problem. It didn't even look that bad.

"Do I try too hard?" she asked suddenly. "Be honest."

Eric rolled over and closed his eyes. Maybe he should have gone with Jackson and Lex.

"I don't think I try too hard," Taylor mused. "I mean, I do try to entertain us, when things get boring. Although Melissa was pretty upset."

Snide responses flew through Eric's head, but he didn't say anything.

Taylor frowned with concern. "You don't think she'd do anything like . . . stupid . . . do you?"

He groaned and sat up. "What answer can I give that will make you go away?"

Pouting, Taylor tied the shirttails together over her T-shirt and looked down to admire her new look. "This isn't horrible," she admitted with a sigh. "Ugh, I can't believe I'm saying this, but I feel guilty about what we did."

"We!" Eric exclaimed. "You're the one who—" Before he could finish, she grabbed his arm and hauled him to his feet. "C'mon."

With Taylor dragging him, they took off in the opposite direction from where Jackson and Lex had gone. *So much for my nap*, Eric thought. *I hope we find her . . . maybe even apologize.*

We've got to find her! Taylor set her jaw with

determination and dragged her reluctant partner into the trees. *She can't stay away, like . . . overnight! That would be, like, gross. And unnecessary, too. All is forgiven, at least on my side. Hostilities are over!*

"Melissa! Where are you?" she called.

If I ran away, people would figure I was being dramatic to prove a point. Or crazy. Maybe nobody would come after me. But Melissa is no drama queen. If she's crazy, it's only because I pushed her over the edge. I . . . I went too far.

"Melissa, come home!" yelled Taylor.

FIVE

"**H**ey! I'm down here!" shouted Melissa. Now her throat was getting sore, and her voice sounded hoarse. She didn't have any water or food, and the afternoon was getting cooler. No matter which way she looked, the overgrown canyon was irritatingly peaceful. And totally uncaring of her plight.

Nobody was even surprised to hear that I have a crush on Jackson. Am I that transparent? Why can't I just shrug problems off, like Jackson does? Would he or Daley have stomped off into the woods, crying, only to fall off a cliff? If I ever get out of this mess alive, I'm going to be tougher and get a thicker skin. And I won't let everybody know what I'm thinking!

First I gotta get help.

She tried to whistle—to save her voice—but she could barely make a squeak. Wouldn't the others realize that she wasn't the kind of person to strike out on her own and become a hermit? Then they would seriously start to look for her. Even if they did, it might take them a day or two, so she had to be mentally prepared to spend the night on this ledge.

Maybe longer than one night.

"Help!" Melissa sat in the dirt, scrunched her back against the cliff wall, and wrapped her arms around her shivering body. The eerie silence of the canyon mocked her feeble shout.

"Melissa!" yelled Jackson as he wandered down the fruit path, looking in every direction. Wasn't this the way she had come? He looked in vain for any sure sign that she had passed this way. The footprints could have been from yesterday.

"Melissa!" called Lex.

Every time either of them yelled, Jackson paused to wait for a response, but there was none. He wanted so badly for Mel to just stroll out of the bushes and give him that goofy smile, but he knew it wasn't likely. They had to admit that this was a big island, and she might not be easy to find. Especially if she didn't want to be found . . . or something had happened to her.

The dangers of this place were something

they didn't think about often enough. They were always so wrapped up in finding food and water, or just trying to get along, that it was easy to forget that this tropical paradise was a wilderness. Their pilot, Captain Russell, and three other kids had already vanished into the interior of this island. They could still return with good news ... or bad. He just didn't want to see Melissa disappear, too.

"Melissa?" yelled Lex helplessly. "Where are you?"

Jackson stopped and bellowed as loudly as he could, "Melissa! *Melissa, come home!*"

Nathan had been digging so hard that he worked up a real sweat, and he put down his shovel and looked at the result of his work. It was a nice pit, about two feet across and two feet deep. Daley had been cutting leaves and twigs from the surrounding trees, and she had a good pile of greenery and stalks.

He picked up one of her branches and placed it across the hole. It fit perfectly. Without a word, Daley started to do the same thing, and they had soon covered the hole with a thin layer of twigs and branches. Then they carefully hid their trap with a sheet of palm fronds, leaves, and grass.

It looked enough like the jungle floor to fool anyone, thought Nathan, even a pig. Plus, they had dug their pit on a narrow part of the trail, where the bushes were overgrown on either side. He felt proud of their work . . . and proud of using his head and not just his brawn, like Jackson would have.

Daley gave him a satisfied smile. "I like it."

Nathan nodded in agreement. "Simple, perfect . . . deadly."

They shook hands, and Daley declared, "Time to start us a pig stampede!"

Eagerly, the two former rivals began to stalk their dinner. It was way too late for lunch, and Nathan's empty stomach fueled his hunting instincts. He looked over at Daley, who gave him a big grin, and he knew that they would be successful. *Who would have thought . . . we're a good team.*

"Melissa-a-a-a!" shouted Taylor.

The marooned cheerleader stumbled along in her sandals, feeling hot, tired, and miserable. She had worn the wrong clothes for search-and-rescue work, and she had brought along the wrong partner. Eric trailed behind her, shuffling and moaning.

"We gotta stop," he rasped. "I'm dying."

"Hello, Melissa!" Taylor yelled. "It's okay, I forgive you!"

Eric groaned and swayed on his feet. "Seriously, Taylor," he said, "I'm still weak."

"Oh, please," Taylor answered. "It's not like I'm having fun, either. Oh, take a rest."

With relief, Eric slumped down on a rock. Taylor had to admit that he looked pretty beat. She paced a few steps into the jungle and looked around, but there was nothing but trees and bugs and uneven terrain that hurt her feet. *Do I even have the right clothes for search-and-rescue?*

Suddenly, she was struck by the selfishness and unfairness of Melissa making her do this. "Why is she being such a drama queen?" Taylor asked, flapping her arms. "I mean, she deserved it. All I did was get even—is that so wrong? It's not like I ruined *her* clothes or anything. I thought about it, but figured it wouldn't be that great of a loss."

Taylor crossed her arms and nodded sagely. "Truth is, I did her a favor! Now Jackson knows she likes him and they can, I don't know . . . be together or something." Taylor winced. "Ugh! Not a good image. Don't you think . . ."

She turned around to look for Eric, but he was gone. His little rock was vacant.

"Eric!" she yelled angrily. Whirling around, she scanned the trees and the path, but he was nowhere to be found. "Hey! Don't leave me out here!"

It was too late to complain, because he had already left her there. Taylor gave a mighty sigh, and she massaged a blister on the heel of her right foot. She had never had a blister before coming to this stupid island, and now she seemed to have them everywhere.

I'm in pain, I'm tired, and I'm farther from the beach than I've ever been, thought Taylor. *But I'm going to find that drama queen and . . . and maybe tell her I went a teensy bit overboard. Then we'll be friends again. If I'm feeling generous, I'll even trade some of my cool clothes for her practical, boring clothes. We'll be like roommates, trading clothes.*

I'll think longer next time . . . before I unleash the full Taylor Revenge Plan.

With her new resolve, Taylor stepped gingerly over the roots and vines and headed into the unknown.

Daley hooted and screeched, and she even did a poor hog call as she chased the squealer between bushes and trees, down the narrow trails of their island paradise. "Piggy! Piggy! Woo-hoo!" she shouted. The afternoon heat unleashed a cloud of humidity from the damp forest, and Daley was seriously sweaty and winded.

"Yaaar!" cried Nathan as he stumbled over a root and plunged into the bushes. "Go . . . pig!"

The pig took an abrupt right turn, narrowly avoiding their trap on the trail. Daley skidded to a stop and dropped to her knees before she fell into the hole, and she panted to catch her breath.

Nathan staggered to his feet and rasped, "The pig's getting smart."

"Yeah, but we can't afford to lose it." Waving

her stick, Daley took off after the beast, trying to corral it back into their ambush. She wasn't going to give up on her idea so easily. Yes, they were shirking all their other chores to do this, but the reward would be worth it. This was an island, and island people ate game like this all the time. *For now, we're island people, and we have to adapt.*

But the pig was so cute, and it seemed to think they were put on this island to play games with it. But survival wasn't a game, and her stomach was gnawing. With grim determination, Daley tried to drive their prey into the pit.

Taylor stumbled and tripped as she plowed through the jungle, and she was glad to come to an open area where there were fewer bushes. In the distance was a tall green mountain, and it seemed like the kind of place an emotional wreck might go. Melissa had definitely been troubled when she left.

"Help!" she yelled, as much for herself as Melissa. "Anybody! I am so lost!"

Oh, why did I let Eric escape? He wasn't any help, but he might have talked me out of going so far. Getting so lost.

With long shadows and a golden hue to the clouds, the mountains grew more and more alluring, and she wandered in that direction. Soon she found herself on a bluff, overlooking an immense canyon, and the awesome beauty caused her to stop dead. This wasn't a good time to admire the scenery, but she had nothing else to look at.

"Where am I?" Taylor yelled at the heavens.

"Hello?" answered a startled voice. "Is somebody there?"

Taylor froze, and her jaw dropped open. She looked around, but she was alone on this windy promontory.

"Melissa?" she asked hesitantly. "Oh, my—"

"Taylor!" answered the voice, sounding giddy.

"Oh, no!" the blond girl shrieked. She stepped closer to the edge of the cliff. "Did . . . did something happen? Are you a ghost?"

"No! I'm down here!"

Taylor could hear the voice beneath her now, and she walked closer to the drop off to look down.

"Be careful," warned the invisible Melissa. "The edge is—"

Before she could finish, Taylor's sandals slipped out from under her, and she found herself on her rump and skidding fast. She screamed and groped for a handhold, but that didn't stop her fall at all. Dirt smeared her face and got under her fingernails as she slid down the steep bank. She would have fallen all the way to the bottom, except for two strong arms that grabbed her.

Taylor got pulled back onto a ledge and into a hollow spot, and she lay gasping in somebody's arms. She turned around to see Melissa, looking grim.

"I got you!" she said.

Taylor glanced over the edge at a plunge that still went hundreds of feet, and she nodded thankfully. "You . . . you're not a ghost?"

"No," Melissa answered. "And I don't plan on being one, either."

Taylor gripped her fluttering stomach and peered over the edge of their perch. So it wasn't a hallucination—they were stranded on a ledge above the Grand Canyon of the South Pacific! She gripped her friend Melissa, just glad to have somebody to hold onto. But the bigger girl staggered, and a clump of dirt crumbled under her feet.

They held onto each other as they tried to find the best place to stand on the terrifying ledge.

Jackson expected to find somebody in the jungle—hopefully Melissa, maybe Daley and Nathan—but he was awfully surprised when he saw Eric shuffling along. Hadn't they left him on the beach, getting his beauty sleep?

"Eric!" shouted Lex excitedly. "Hey, Eric!"

The skinny kid stopped and waited for Jackson and Lex to surround him. "What are you doing out here?" Lex asked.

He shrugged. "Taylor and I came looking for Melissa." He turned to Jackson and added, "I'm not a total jerk. But I'm still weak, man. I gotta get back."

Jackson stepped past Eric and peered down the trail. "So where's Taylor?"

"Hmmm?" Eric turned around as if he expected her to be right behind him. "Still looking, I guess. We got separated—thought she was behind me." He continued shuffling down the path.

"Now we gotta find both of them," complained Lex.

Jackson nodded grimly and yelled, "Melissa! Taylor!" When there was no answer, he plodded deeper into the interior and waved for Lex to follow him.

On the ledge, Taylor tried to hold onto Melissa's arm, but the Asian-American girl gently pushed her away. Taylor felt dirt slipping under her feet, and she gasped as she pressed herself against the rock.

"What . . . what if this breaks?" she asked in panic.

Melissa scowled and answered, "It's not gonna break. If it does . . . we won't have a lot of time to think about it."

"But what if nobody finds us?" Taylor muttered. "I don't want to die here." She paused in thought, then added, "I don't want to die anywhere!"

"They'll find us . . . sooner or later," Melissa said with a sigh. "I trust Jackson. And Nathan and Daley and Lex."

Taylor waited for her to keep naming names,

but she didn't. The blond girl put her hands on her hips and said, "Hel-lo! I'm the one who found you."

Melissa glared at her. "Yeah, but I'm not a big fan of yours right now."

Taylor gulped and tried to back away, but there wasn't any room on the crumbling rock. An apology was about to cross her lips, but it froze on her tongue. In the middle of this life-and-death crisis, it would be kind of stupid to go all gushy. *Here I am, about to die, and I'm stuck on a ledge with somebody who hates me. And look at all the dirt under my fingernails!*

She tightened her shirttails, and Melissa blinked at her. "You're wearing the shirt."

"Yeah," admitted Taylor. "When I tie it like this, it's not totally hideous."

Melissa leaned back against the rock and looked at her feet. "I knew you'd be mad when I told you what happened, but I didn't think you'd go all viper like that. I mean, what you did was pretty rotten."

Taylor almost lashed into Melissa. But going ballistic out here on this ledge would be as stupid as going all mushy. She was done fighting. At least for this lousy day. "I don't like it when people mess with my things," Taylor explained simply.

"Oh, so you fight back by messing with their lives?" Melissa asked, shaking her head. "What are you gonna do if something *really* bad happens to you?"

Taylor opened her mouth to respond, but nothing really bad had happened to her . . . until she got stuck on this stupid island. Now it was hard to tell the good times from the bad times, because they all involved eating seafood and getting rashes. Maybe all of them were getting punished for not being nice enough in that other paradise . . . their old life.

"I'll think of something," she muttered. Taylor peered at the darkening sky, and her lower lip trembled. "Help!" she screamed.

SIX

"I think I heard something," Lex said, gazing across an overgrown meadow toward the distant mountains. "It was faint but maybe—"

Kneeling on the ground, Jackson pointed to a sandal track in the mud. "Yeah, and there are footprints here, too. It must be them. These flip-flop tracks . . . Taylor for sure."

He jumped to his feet and began to run across the rugged terrain. When he spotted something white—maybe clothing—he knew he was on the right track.

"Melissa!" he shouted.

"Taylor!" yelled Lex as he struggled to keep up with Jackson. "Where are you?"

They climbed to the top of the rise and were greeted with the sight of an enormous canyon full of deep shadows and slate-gray waterfalls. It made Jackson feel as if he were nothing on this island. Just another ant on a leaf.

"Wow!" Lex said in amazement, but there was no time to admire the view. Jackson spotted Melissa's jacket on the edge of the bluff—it looked like a sheer drop-off.

Oh, no, he thought in panic. "Melissa!"

On the chilly ledge, the shadows were deepening, and so were Taylor's spirits. Melissa was being tough and brave, but then she had been on the ledge all afternoon. For her, the novelty was over. *Maybe I'm past the denial stage and into that bad stage*, Taylor thought nervously. *The one where you know you're going to die.*

I have to apologize, she decided. *I can't die with the shirt affair on my conscience.* "I'd like to—" she began.

"Melissa!" called a male voice from above, drowning out her words.

"Hey! We're down here!" Taylor was so excited that she jumped . . . and nearly fell off the crumbling edge. Only Melissa's quick reaction to grab her shoulder and pull her back saved her skin.

"Be careful!" Melissa shouted, looking upward. "The edge isn't safe!"

After a few tense moments, a head peaked over the rim—it was Jackson! He was wisely crawling on his belly, with most of his weight on safe ground.

"Are you all right?" he asked with concern. "Are you safe?"

"We're okay," Melissa answered with a grateful smile. "Be careful!"

"But get us out," Taylor added. "Please!"

"Listen," he said, "Lex will stay with you while I get the rope. I'll be as fast as I can."

With that, he was gone. The relieved survivors started to hug each other, before they remembered they were quarreling.

"I'm not supposed to go near the edge!" Lex shouted. "But it's okay, I'm up here."

"Yeah, it's okay," Taylor breathed with relief. She looked at Melissa, hoping she would get a smile, but her former friend was still ticked.

"You were right," Taylor said apologetically, "they came."

Melissa nodded as if she had known it all along. "Some people you can count on."

Daley heaved a weary sigh and slumped onto a log, exhausted from chasing the wild pig around half the jungle. They had run everywhere, except where the trap was dug. Nathan was keeping Porky in view, but that wasn't difficult since the animal took a break every time they did. Daley was sure the pig was enjoying this sport more than the humans.

"Not a good feeling," Nathan whispered, "being outsmarted by a pig." But he still sounded as if he was having fun. Daley figured that hunting beat drudge survival chores any day.

Daley nodded wearily, because their prey was only about ten yards away from their trap. But it looked as if the two would never meet.

Suddenly, a wild figure came crashing through the jungle, running at full speed like Tarzan. His dramatic entrance startled the pig and made it scoot down the path . . . right toward their trap. Daley glanced at the runner, who looked like Jackson, then back at the squealer just before it dropped through their camouflage of leaves and branches into the waiting pit.

Nathan gasped in delight, and Daley whirled around to thank Jackson—but he was gone. She didn't think he had even seen them. She and Nathan gave each other a high five and ran over to inspect their prize.

Oooh, that's a fat little pig, Daley thought, now that she got a closer look. It was also a very panicked and pathetic creature, and it knew that the chase was over. This was real life now, not a game. Daley's heart went out to the frightened beast, but, after all, it *was* a food source. *We need protein, and I have to be on the side of the hungry people, not the unlucky dinner.*

Flashing on the same thought, Daley and Nathan both looked over at the ice cooler and the object sitting on top of it—the butcher knife.

Melissa wrung her hands nervously. There was barely enough room on the narrow ledge to breathe, but she was trying to stay calm in order to keep Taylor calm. It took longer than expected for Jackson to return with the rope, and the ledge *was* beginning to crumble. She didn't need to say anything to Taylor—they both knew as they huddled closer together.

Unseen, Lex kept talking to them from above, trying to cheer them up. The drop beneath their feet was just as steep as ever. *We may have company, but we're still in danger*, thought Melissa. Plus, it was getting cold on the windy ledge, and the shadows had deepened in the canyon until they looked like rivers of ink coursing through rugged emeralds.

Finally, she heard Jackson's voice, which made Melissa feel a lot better. For a moment, she even returned Taylor's desperate smile.

"Rope coming down!" Jackson called. Staying away from the lip of the canyon, he cautiously lowered a line down to them. "One of you put it under your arms, and we'll pull you up."

Melissa grabbed their end, which was already tied in a loop, and offered it to Taylor. "You go first."

The blonde suddenly waved her arms and went into full panic mode. "No way. I can't do this."

"Yeah, you can," Melissa insisted.

She began to shake. "N . . . no, I'll fall. I'm scared of heights and—"

"Taylor!" Melissa shouted at her. They were nose to nose, and Melissa stared into the shorter girl's pale blue eyes. It sounded like someone else's voice coming from her mouth, mixed with Jackson's no-nonsense tone. "Put the rope on and go."

Shocked at her bluntness, Taylor nodded dumbly. The girl stood still while Melissa put the loop over her head and under her arms.

"We'll pull, you climb!" Jackson shouted. The rope went taut, making Taylor gasp with alarm.

Melissa grabbed her arm and helped her find a good foothold in the rock. Taylor whimpered as she began to climb. "Good! You got it!" Melissa said encouragingly.

She didn't know how many people were pulling—maybe it was only Jackson and Lex—but Taylor slowly scrabbled her way up the cliff face. The cheerleader carefully hid her athletic ability most of the time, but she could scramble when her life was in danger. She struggled near the top, and clods of dirt tumbled down on Melissa. She covered her head and pressed against the cliff wall.

Finally, Jackson leaned over and grabbed Taylor. When her head, body, and then legs disappeared over the rim of the canyon, Melissa let out her breath. She heard Taylor squealing excitedly, and she had to smile.

Even if I'm an emotional wreck sometimes, Melissa thought, *at least I keep my head in a crisis.*

"You okay?" Jackson shouted as he lowered the rope back down to her.

"Yeah," she answered with a smile. "I am now."

They pulled her to the top without any problems, and Melissa wanted to give Jackson a big hug. But she settled for giving Lex a little hug. In silence and exhaustion, they walked back to their camp on the beach, while the sun slowly retreated from the golden-hued sky. The night birds began to chortle, and shadows twisted through the tall trees.

"See anything interesting out there?" asked Jackson.

Melissa frowned in thought. "Well," she began, "I saw something. On the other side of the canyon. Maybe not."

"What?"

"I thought it was a person. It was too far away to tell for sure." Melissa shrugged at his puzzled expression. Jackson looked as if he wanted to say more, but she was too ragged out for any kind of conversation. Especially a serious one. She slowed her step and fell back to walk beside Lex.

Nathan gripped the knife in his hand while he looked down at the helpless pig trapped in the hole. It was caught in some of the vines, and flies were buzzing around its head. The animal squealed and looked sadly at them. "Aren't you my friends?" the pig seemed to ask. "Weren't we playing just a few minutes ago?"

With a gulp, Nathan glanced at Daley. She was cringing as much as he was. "We have to do it," she insisted.

"Yeah." Nathan shook his head miserably. "Man, who knew the trip would come down to something like this? Do you want to flip a coin?"

"You or me," she answered glumly. "It doesn't make any difference."

"Ready?" Nathan lifted the butcher knife over his head.

Daley nodded grimly. "Let's do it."

Sucking in his breath, Nathan swept the knife downward . . . toward the creature trapped in the pit. At the last second, he changed direction and plunged the knife into the ground. Daley blinked at him in surprise and smiled. Nathan knew they were on the same wave.

With relief, he said, "Let's get him out. One . . . two . . . three . . . *now*!" At the same time, they reached into the pit and grabbed a chunk of squirming pig. With some difficulty, they hauled the little squealer out of the hole and set him on the ground. He promptly scampered away into the bushes, and Nathan and Daley laughed at each other.

"You know," Daley said, "we ought to take a look at the roots and stuff he was eating. If a pig can eat it, a human probably can, too."

"Grubs and roots," Nathan said, "yum, yum." He turned serious for a moment. "You know, Jackson would have killed him."

Daley shrugged and wiped the dirt off her shorts. "Maybe. Maybe not. Maybe three months from now, no pig on the island will be safe from any of us. Don't worry about what Jackson does or doesn't do. Just do what you do."

"Like ... let dinner get away," Nathan said with a scowl.

"Hey, so we're not to the point of killing ... yet." Daley cuffed him on the cheek and strode off into the forest, anxious to get back to camp and see why Jackson was running like a maniac.

The light was fading, and the surf had taken on that bronze-purple tone that looked so regal. No wonder the ancient kings always wanted to turn back the surf, thought Melissa; they identified with the royal colors at twilight. From the canyon, she had smelled the ocean, but now the salty mist was in her face again.

At the end of the day, Jackson was still working on his solo project. And he looked determined to finish. Melissa watched him arrange rocks for a few seconds before she worked up the courage to approach him.

"Hi," she said.

He looked up and gave her a smile. "Hey, I've got something for you." He reached into a pile of dirty clothes and held up a small black object. It took Melissa a moment to realize that it was a tape from the video camera. *My tape.*

Jackson handed it to her and said, "You should keep that in a safe place."

"Oh, I will," Melissa assured him with a nervous laugh. The conversation was turning awkward, and she looked around for a way to escape gracefully. All the secrets were out in the open now, and it was hard not to trip over them. In one way, Melissa was relieved. In another, it felt as if she had learned one of those life lessons that really hurt. It made her feel older.

Jackson cleared his throat and said, "Listen, uh, since we've all got to live with each other here, I think it would be kind of weird for any of us to . . . you know—"

Although she expected it, Melissa didn't want to get the brush-off right now. So close to the pain. "It's okay," she answered, almost running down the beach. "Please forget this ever happened! I'm so embarrassed—I know we're just friends."

"But after we get back home," Jackson said, "maybe I can call you. Or something?"

Melissa stopped dead in her tracks, and she tried not to squeal with happiness. That was more like it. Not a brush-off, but hope for the future. *If only our future wasn't the biggest secret of all.*

Nonchalantly, Melissa turned around and said,

"I'd like that. Any ideas on how to get rescued?"

Jackson laughed. "Give me a hand here."

Melissa nodded and picked up one of his rocks. Working together, they finished laying the stones on this lonely stretch of beach. The rocks spelled "H . . . E . . . L . . . P" in letters big enough for the whole world to see.

From the girls' tent, Daley watched Jackson and Melissa working on their "HELP" sign, and she saw Eric and Taylor resting by the campfire. Apparently, she and Nathan had missed a bunch of excitement today. People falling off cliffs? Bringing home a dead pig wouldn't have topped that.

Okay, we took a day off, but we learned something about ourselves. Sometimes just the teamwork alone is worth the effort, even if the end isn't how you planned it.

Daley turned on the video camera and began her diary.

Daley

I think survival means a lot of things. Mostly it's about strength and luck. In the short time we've been here, it's getting really clear who's got the goods . . . and who doesn't.

Daley shook her head and pushed the pause button. She didn't want to sound negative. Hadn't she and Nathan failed to bring home dinner when it was right in their hands? All of them were making mistakes and getting on one another's nerves, but they were still a team.

Taylor and Eric are not with the program. They seem to think this is still high school, where popularity and selfishness are cool. Maybe tomorrow they will get it. Melissa seems okay, back to her usual self. Sometimes it's good to let a secret escape. Or a pig.

Daley wondered more about how Jackson was taking it, because he was a really private dude. When Eric played Mel's confession for Taylor, he was getting his own revenge . . . on Jackson.

Even Nathan, who was overconfident most of the time, was jealous of Jackson. There was still that bad blood between them from when they almost got into a fight. In fact, none of the boys were jelling into friends. Except for Lex, but her brother was too young to be any kind of threat to their egos. *Oh well, this is a problem for another day.*

Daley restarted the camera and finished her diary.

Daley

Until we get rescued, we have to do all we can to survive. But in the end, we also have to be able to live with ourselves.

SEVEN

The next day, Eric still felt guilty about punking Melissa and spilling her secret. Plus, he felt better physically. Good enough to actually do some work. Even so, he wasn't going back to that stupid water-hauling job, no matter how guilty he felt. There were limits to his goodness. Nor was he going to volunteer to help Jackson, who was still pretty ticked off. Let Action Jackson do his own work.

Nathan was always doing something kind of fun. Or crazy. Eric found his bud on the main path, heading into the jungle. "Whatcha doing?" he asked. "Need any help?"

"Same old grind," answered Nathan. "Collecting fruit."

That didn't sound too harsh, so Eric nodded. "Count me in."

"Get yourself a towel or a blanket or something," Nathan said, "to carry the goodies. If you put the fruit in a sling, your hands are still free."

"I'm following you, chief," Eric answered good-naturedly. "Whatever you do, I'll do."

An hour later, he regretted his eagerness, because they didn't do anything but walk for an hour. They finally found a few decent specimens of fruit, but only a few. After walking another hour deeper into the jungle, Nathan's sling was half full and Eric's had one bruised mango in it.

Not only that, but Nathan plunged ahead through the thickets, leaving Eric struggling to catch up. For the tenth time that day, Nathan pushed back a branch and let it swing free, and it smacked Eric right in the face.

If we're gonna play the Three Stooges, I want to be Moe, he decided.

Loudly, Eric complained, "We came this far from camp because?"

"Because we gotta find every possible source of fruit," Nathan answered. "If we want more, we have to go farther away to find it. I've been keeping track—we've never gone this far in this direction."

"I can see why." Eric held up his pitiful mango.

"We don't want to run out," Nathan insisted.

"Right. Fruit doesn't grow on trees, you know." Eric chuckled at his own joke, but his friend remained stone-faced and focused. "It was a joke. Lighten up," added Eric.

Nathan finally stopped for a moment to survey

the leafy branches all around them. "If we were smart, we'd start a garden."

"No, we're not that smart," Eric said quickly. "I don't want to even think about being here that long."

"Neither do I, but I'd rather be safe than—"

"Whoa, wait!" Eric exclaimed, cutting him off. He peered at a tree in the distance—at something that shouldn't be there. "I thought you said nobody's been out this far?"

"They haven't. Not that I know of."

"Then what's that?" Eric pointed to a scrawny tree standing among several others of its kind, but this one had a clear hint of red on its trunk.

As soon as he saw the jarring color, Nathan took off running, and Eric followed right behind him. As they got closer, Eric realized it wasn't paint or a bit of cloth stuck in the tree—it was a blazing red strip of cloth *tied* to the trunk. Not only that, but the knot held a tattered slip of paper, folded in two.

Eric and Nathan looked at each other, then at the knotted cloth. "So?" Eric asked.

Nathan carefully untied the cloth and the message. "None of us has been out here," he whispered.

"So what's that?"

"It's proof"—he unfolded the note and held out the paper to Eric—"that we're not alone."

Scrawled on the page in block letters was the word "HELP."

Daley looked around the camp and saw that it was good. Lex was on top of the wrecked plane, adding a ten-foot-tall bamboo mast to their radio antenna, hoping to boost the signal some more. Jackson was over at the fire pit, boiling water and cracking coconuts. Nathan and Eric were off somewhere, gathering fruit.

Taylor was missing in action, but maybe she was entitled to a break after finding Melissa and falling over the edge of a cliff. The sun was high in the sky but covered by a slight overcast, which made it cool and pleasant in the salty breeze.

"Are you ready to get another one?" Mel asked, stepping from behind the airplane.

"Yes, let's do it," Daley said.

The two girls climbed into the cabin of the plane and went back to a project they had started that morning. With wrenches and screwdrivers, they attacked one of the passenger seats and loosened it from the slats on the floor. With some difficulty, they picked up the airplane seat and carried it toward the door.

"This is so smart," Melissa said.

"Really," agreed Daley. "I'm so tired of sitting in sand all the time."

As they passed a section of the bulkhead, Melissa stopped suddenly and said, "Oh, wait." They set down the seat, and Melissa peered at an open panel under one of the windows. "Look!"

Daley followed her gaze until she spotted it, too—something shiny on the edge of the hole. "What is it?" she asked.

Melissa reached for the prize. "I think it's a—" As her fingers touched the object, it dropped out of sight behind the bulkhead. "No!" she exclaimed. "It *was* a necklace. It fell down there."

Daley assessed the situation and decided that the space behind the panel had to be pretty small. She had just the right tool in their bag of odds and ends.

"No problem." She opened her bag and grabbed a length of wire with a hook on the end. Daley stuck the bent end down into the hole and fished around for a few seconds. Finally, she heard a scraping sound and felt a slight tug, and she knew she had snagged something.

"Ta-da!" she exclaimed as she rescued the necklace.

"Yes!" echoed Melissa.

It was an eye-catching piece of jewelry—a beautiful necklace made of coral, amethyst, and silver—and it looked expensive. "Wow, it's beautiful!" Daley said.

"Whose is it?" Mel asked.

Daley shook her head. "I don't know, I've never seen it before. Who was sitting in that seat?"

Melissa shrugged. Both of them gently handled the necklace, and Melissa said, "It really is pretty. What should we do with it?"

Daley knew what *she* wanted to do with it—put it on. She couldn't claim the necklace outright, because it probably belonged to Taylor, who owned enough jewelry for ten girls. *Melissa spotted it, but I rescued it,* she thought.

"What if it belongs to someone who's not here?" Mel asked. "Like one of the kids who went with Captain Russell?"

Daley smiled. "We'll keep it nice and safe."

Jackson found a way to kill two birds with one coconut by using the giant seed as a hammer to pound tent stakes. If the shell cracked while he pounded away, that was great—he had a coconut ready for eating. If the stake got set in the ground, that was okay, too.

He heard shouts and commotion, and he looked up to see Nathan and Eric come charging out of the jungle. "Hey!" Nathan shouted. "You gotta see this!"

"I'm the one who found it!" Eric claimed.

Jackson heaved a sigh and set down the coconut, wondering what had gotten them so excited. Nathan showed him a tattered note.

"It was tied to a tree by a piece of cloth," Nathan explained.

"Red cloth," Eric added. "That's why I saw it."

"We left the marker so we can find it again," Nathan said.

Jackson studied the note, which had one word on it, "HELP." He frowned in thought and handed the sheet back to Nathan. "Who put it there?" he asked.

"That's the point," Nathan answered. "None of us. It's too far out."

"It must be from the pilot and the others," Jackson guessed.

Eric shrugged. "Maybe. Or maybe somebody else is on the island."

With a frown, Jackson looked again at the crude message. He always thought that finding other people on the island would be a lucky break, but now he wasn't so sure. The people who hung out on a deserted island might not be the kind of people they wanted to meet. Nature wasn't the only force that could be dangerous.

"Either way," Nathan said, "somebody's out there. And somebody's in trouble."

Daley thought she had seen everything in the week or so they had been stranded, but she wasn't ready for what she saw at the girls' tent. Taylor had dragged all their sleeping bags into a big pile, and she had a bottle of water, which she was about to dump on them.

"Stop!" Daley called. She and Melissa dropped the airplane seats they had been carrying and rushed toward the blonde. "What are you doing?"

Taylor looked at Daley as if she had two heads. "No offense, but it's getting rank in that tent. These sleeping bags need a good rinse."

Again she started to pour water on them, but Daley grabbed the bottle. "No! You don't wash sleeping bags."

"Not unless you want them to smell like old sneakers," Melissa added.

"But they, like . . . reek!" Taylor protested.

"So you air them out," Daley said. She grabbed all the sleeping bags and carried them to her clothesline.

"That better work," Taylor said with a pout, "because I am, like, gagging in there."

When Daley returned, Melissa was showing Taylor the necklace they had rescued from the plane. "Look what I found."

Taylor's eyes widened with interest as she studied the elegant piece of jewelry. "Wow!"

"Is it yours?" Mel asked hesitantly.

"I wish," Taylor muttered. Then she smiled and said, "I mean, yes . . . yes it is!"

"Yeah, right." Daley stepped up and snatched the necklace from the blond girl. "We haven't decided what to do with it yet."

Melissa winced and looked as though she was choosing her words carefully. "Actually, I was thinking that—since I found it—I should keep it."

Daley scowled and said, "Uh, that's not a given. I'm the one who got it out of the plane, remember?"

"But I found it," Melissa protested. "Finders keepers, right?"

"Breaking news . . . that's not a real law," Daley said.

Melissa narrowed her eyes at the redhead. "C'mon, Daley! Can't you let somebody else have their way for once?"

"What do you mean?" she asked. "I don't always get my way!"

"Well, yeah you do," Melissa snapped.

Daley put her hands on her hips and said, "I so resent that!"

"But it's true," Melissa insisted. "I'm not gonna let you bully me this time. I think the necklace should be *mine*."

"Bully?" Daley replied, narrowing her eyes. Mel's new attitude was overdue, but she was wrong! "Well, you know what?" Daley said. "I think it should be *mine*!"

While they argued, Taylor slipped between them and calmly grabbed the necklace. She smiled and said, "Until you kids settle this, I'll keep it safe."

Daley and Melissa were still glaring at each other. "You are so unfair!" Melissa said.

"And you are so juvenile!"

"I don't believe you said that!" Melissa crossed her arms and glared at Daley.

"I don't believe you're such a baby!" Daley whirled around, looking for Taylor, but the blond girl was halfway to the tent with *her* necklace.

"Hey!" a voice called. Daley turned again and saw Lex running toward them. "Important meeting at the fire pit! C'mon!"

The girls glared at each other, then followed the ten-year-old to the gathering. The boys were already present, and Taylor appeared a moment later, *wearing* the disputed necklace. Melissa stared at Daley as if this horrible outcome had been *her* fault.

Daley was distracted by her anger, until Jackson said, "It looks like somebody else is on this island. Have any of you seen this note before?"

He nodded to Nathan, who handed around the sheet they had found in the woods. "We found it beyond the northwest fruit trail," Nathan said, "past the kiwis. Did any of you put it there?"

When no one answered, Eric said, "I was the one who found it!"

"Let one person tell it," Jackson suggested.

Nathan ended his story about the red cloth tied to the tree by saying, "Bottom line . . . somebody's out there."

Eric cleared his throat and waved his hat. "Did I mention that *I* was the one who found it?"

Lex frowned in thought and said what all of them were thinking. "It might be Captain Russell and the others."

"If it is," Taylor answered with a thoughtful pout, "that means he got them lost . . . again."

"They must have gotten farther than that in eight days," Daley said. But she couldn't think of a better explanation.

Melissa looked worriedly at Jackson and the others. "Whoever it is, they need help."

Almost everyone nodded in agreement, and Jackson pointed to the forest. "Let's go take a look around."

"Great," Nathan said. "We can start where we found the note."

"Where *I* found the note," Eric insisted.

Jackson pointed to the youngest among them. "Lex, stay here in case somebody shows up."

"Got it." He almost saluted.

"But keep out of sight," Eric warned. "We don't know who or *what* is out there."

"Don't try to scare the kid," Daley said. "Lex knows how to keep watch. He's always been good at spying on *me*."

The boy grinned and promised, "I'll be alert."

Jackson turned to Daley and asked, "How many search groups do you think we'll need?"

"Two," she answered. "We need lots of eyes on both teams. You can take Eric and Taylor, and I'll take—"

"Uh . . . that doesn't work for me," Melissa blurted.

"Excuse me?" Daley asked, putting her hands on her hips.

"What if I don't want to be in your group?" Melissa matched her angry gaze.

Daley snapped, "Oh please! Would you stop being such a baby!" Now Melissa had gone too far with this punk attitude.

Melissa looked shocked. "Then stop being so bossy," she countered.

The two of them stalked off toward the jungle, and Taylor laughed. "Me-ow!"

EIGHT

Daley

I really don't care about the dumb necklace.
I'm just tired of protecting Melissa from
getting her feelings hurt.

**Daley frowned in disappointment and turned
off the video camera.**

Melissa

Daley really hurt my feelings. This was about
a dumb necklace, but now she's made it
personal.

**Melissa snorted in anger and couldn't think of
any more to say to her diary.**

Jackson hung back to let Eric and Nathan lead the search party to the tree where they'd found the note. He glanced at Daley, who was a step ahead of him, then back at Melissa, who was two steps behind him. Both of them were still fuming, and he had yet to figure out why. There had been no time to pull them aside and find out what was going on, and their feud worried him.

He counted on Melissa and Daley to keep their heads and be there to get things done. Plus, they would have to take charge if anything happened to him. Danger was all around them, in forms they may not even know about, and none of them were immune to accident. Or worse. He didn't worry about the others as long as Daley and Melissa were around.

So now they were feuding, and Taylor was humming cheerfully as she fingered a new necklace around her pretty neck. *What is going on here?*

This was a craggy part of the island, with rocky terrain and sharp scraggly plants. No wonder they didn't come here looking for food. In time, Eric led them into a clearing, then suddenly stopped and looked around. Plodding to a halt, Jackson and the girls gathered around him, and Eric pointed to a grove of saplings. "It was this way," he said with certainty.

As they started off, Eric stopped and pointed in another direction. "No, that way." He changed his mind again. "Or maybe over there. I remember that tree, but it looks the same as *that* tree. Maybe it's—"

"Hey!" a voice called. Now all of them turned in the same direction to see Nathan at the top of the ridge . . . leaning against a tree trunk decorated with a red ribbon.

"That's what I thought," Eric said. "That way."

Jackson led the charge to the tree, and the story became more real when he saw the torn piece of cloth flapping from the slender trunk. Someone must have been very desperate, very lost, to leave a note way out here. They couldn't have expected to get much help.

Everyone stared solemnly at the marked tree until Nathan said, "It looks like it was ripped from a shirt."

"How do we know which way to look?" Mel asked. She stuck her hands in her pockets and surveyed the unfamiliar stretch of forest.

Jackson did the same, and he finally said, "Well, they aren't on the way back to camp. How about one group goes east, and the other goes west?"

"Good," Nathan answered. "I'll go east. Who's with me?"

"I'll go," Taylor volunteered. She began walking, but nobody followed her.

"Uh . . . that's west," Daley called.

Taylor did an about-face and marched back toward them. "Just testing," she said cheerfully.

Daley rolled her eyes and turned to Jackson. "I'll babysit Taylor. You babysit Melissa."

Melissa scowled at the redhead. "You are so mean!" She looked pointedly at Jackson then struck out toward the east. Jackson motioned to Eric to come with him, and he jogged to catch up with Melissa.

He wanted to ask her what was going on, but he knew better than to interrogate an irate woman. Suppose she told him, and it was worse than he imagined? Besides, his own relationship with Melissa had been strained lately, and it wasn't as if they were talking a lot about their feelings.

"Hello!" he yelled, remembering why they had trekked deep into the jungle. "Anybody out there?"

Melissa slowed down her angry walk and took a deep breath. She scanned the trees and shouted, "Hey! We're here to help you!"

Eric looked around and wrinkled his nose. "They're not here. Let's keep going." He strode ahead of them, leaving Jackson alone with Melissa for the first time that day.

"What's the deal with you and Daley?" he whispered.

"Nothing," she answered, tight-lipped. "Except that I totally hate her right now."

Jackson nodded and backed away. "Oh. Glad it's nothing."

"She thinks she's intimidating me," Melissa

grumbled, "but she's not. At least not a lot." With that, she turned and marched after Eric.

I don't even want the stupid necklace, Daley thought as she trudged through the sticky underbrush. *But there's a principle here. I'm not gonna give it to Melissa just because I feel sorry for her. We're in survival mode. She's gotta toughen up. I'm just doing her a favor.*

"Yoo-hoo!" Taylor called. "Anybody out there?"

Nathan stopped to study the damp ground. "I don't see any tracks. Should we split up?"

"No," Daley answered quickly. "We're split up enough."

Daley stopped replaying her fight with Melissa in her mind, and she gazed around this unfamiliar part of the forest. There were no trails, just plants that wanted to scratch her knees and leave burrs in her socks. If somebody else was out here, there had to be some sign of them.

Then she spotted it—in a distant stand of trees—a flash of red. "There!" she called.

Daley led the way, with Nathan following right behind and Taylor meandering along. It was the red cloth, holding a note tied to a tree, just like the first one. She pulled out the note and opened it.

Just like the first one, it read: "HELP."

"We're going the right way," Nathan said with confidence.

Taylor caught up with them and asked, "But is this the way they came from? Or the way they went to?"

Nathan and Daley laughed at her twisted logic, until they thought about it a bit more. Nathan frowned and said, "You know, she's right."

Daley shook her head, unable to deal with Taylor's having a good point. It was true. They could be going farther away from whoever needed help, but they had to keep looking.

"Let's just keep going," she said, picking a direction and heading there. "Hello! Can anyone hear me?"

"Hey!" Nathan shouted. "Is anyone there?"

"Yeah, we're busy!" Taylor shouted. "If you're here, let us know!" Nathan turned around and found Taylor smiling at him. Now that Daley and Melissa were feuding over whatever, she was contented. And there was something different about the way she looked, too. A little more sparkle.

Nathan shook his head and tried to keep up with Daley.

"You don't want to talk about it?" Jackson asked in a low voice. At times, he had to jog to catch Melissa as she blazed a trail downhill, and they had left Eric far behind.

"What's to talk about?" she snapped. "Daley is just a control freak. You could see that in high school, but out here . . ." She put her head down and scowled. "I don't want to talk about it."

"Okay, but at least slow down," Jackson said. "Eric needs to catch up and we're in low ground here."

"I'll look for tracks," she agreed, coming to a halt and surveying the area. "There's some bamboo, so it must be wet there. I'll check it out."

"Cool." Jackson gave her a smile, but she didn't smile back.

He wandered away from her, looking for broken branches. Jackson yelled a few times, and Eric joined in the shouting. But the important cry came a moment later.

"Hey! Over here!" Melissa yelled. She waved to them from a marshy area near a stand of bamboo, and Jackson and Eric ran to take a look. Melissa pointed to a very small footprint. "Look."

Jackson bent down to study the tread. "It's a hiking boot. It might be a girl, or a small guy."

"Or a big guy with creepy-small feet," Eric said.

Melissa and Jackson looked at each other and cringed. Eric added, "You know, Melissa, you're very observant. Just like me!"

Jackson tried to ignore him as he concentrated on the footprint. "It's pointed this way."

Melissa nodded, and Jackson blazed the way

through the thick brush. He wasn't going to think anymore about feuds or the million other things about his fellow survivors that drove him crazy. They had to find whoever was out here, or they would never sleep well again.

Nathan heard a frustrated grunt, and he turned around to see that Taylor was having a hard time negotiating some fallen logs. He stopped his trek through the jungle to take her arm and steady her as she climbed over the branches. It didn't help that she always wore the most useless shoes.

"Thanks," she said, with honest relief.

That's when he noticed what was different about her. "Hey, cool necklace. You been hiding that?"

Daley veered out of her way in order to pass them. "Don't get used to it," she told Taylor. With a squinty-eyed glare, Daley moved on.

Nathan looked quizzically at Taylor, and she lowered her voice to say, "It's better you don't know."

She patted him on the shoulder and followed Daley. Nathan decided she was right, and he gazed up at the treetops. The smell of rain was in the air, and the sky was darkening. He sure hoped they found their mystery visitor before the weather got nasty, or they might all be lost in this wilderness.

Jackson stopped and surveyed a seemingly endless expanse of rugged terrain and prickly underbrush, all of it looking exactly like what they had just passed. Even with a compass, he wasn't sure they had been heading east or were following the footprints. At this point, they were just stumbling around.

Melissa also looked winded and frustrated. The only one who seemed undaunted was Eric, but the smile faded from his face when he caught up with them.

"Uh-oh," he said, gazing into the distance.

"What?" Jackson asked.

"You don't see it? More red." As soon as Eric pointed, they all saw the vibrant cloth tied to a branch, only this time there was no note attached.

Jackson led the stampede to a spot under a tree where some branches and palm fronds were piled, as if to make a crude shelter. His dread grew with every step closer, because there was clearly something lying under the tree . . . under the red cloth. Then he saw a hand sticking from the woodpile—a delicate hand with a ring on it.

"Oh, man," Melissa said worriedly. "Hello! Are you okay?" she shouted, but there was no answer.

Jackson stopped Eric and said, "Go get the others. Fast."

"Me?" he protested. "Why can't Melissa—?"

"Go!" Jackson ordered.

Eric nodded and took off, and Melissa shook her head at Jackson. "I'm scared," she admitted.

"Then wait here." Jackson wished he didn't have to go any closer. They both knew it could be a dead body. From the slender build and long hair, it sure looked like a girl under that tree.

"No chance." Melissa led the way toward the body, and Jackson took a deep breath and followed her.

NINE

"**H**ello!" Melissa shouted again as they got closer to the still figure lying in the jungle. Yelling was pointless, thought Jackson. Whoever it was, they were unconscious . . . or worse.

When they reached the spot, he saw she was lying on her face. He recognized what was left of the red shirt—from the bits of cloth tied to the trees—but he couldn't remember who else had long black hair. He held his breath as he reached down, took her slender shoulder, and turned her over.

Melissa gasped. "It's Abby!"

Abby was a pretty Asian-American. Last seen, she was marching off with their pilot to look for help. That was about nine days ago. *What did they find out there?* Jackson wondered.

He didn't know Abby very well—no better than he had known the others before getting stranded with them. Despite the sunburn and dirt and bruises, she still looked attractive. He checked her pulse to see how urgent the situation was. To his surprise, he felt the steady pumping of blood. To make sure, he bent really close to her mouth and nose.

Melissa twisted her hands nervously. "Is she—?"

"She's breathing," he answered.

Melissa let out a relieved breath. "What do you think happened?" she asked. "Where are the others? Her backpack is gone! Why is she alone? What did the—"

"Let's worry about all that later, okay?" Jackson said, feeling frustrated.

"Right. Right. Of course."

Jackson gently touched the girl's cheek and said, "Abby? C'mon, Abby. Wake up, please."

When she didn't respond, he looked helplessly at Melissa. "I don't know what to do."

The girl nodded gravely, and Jackson hoped her hidden healer was about to take over again. After all, she had saved Eric's life while the rest of them stood around and panicked. "Okay, okay," Melissa said, collecting her thoughts. "She needs water."

Quickly, Jackson opened a water bottle and poured some on her lips, but Abby wasn't going to drink anything in this condition. "She's out of it," he muttered.

"We should get her back to camp," Melissa said.

"I don't see her bleeding or anything," he answered. "She's breathing okay. Let's wait a few minutes for the others."

Melissa nodded grimly.

Eric had never run so fast in his entire life, and he was able to retrace his team's steps from all the muddy footprints they had left. In no time, he reached the tree with the original red cloth, and he flew past it and dashed in the direction Daley's team had gone.

Following their shouts, he located the other search group in short time. "Hey! Hey!" he shouted, waving like a maniac. "Here I am!"

Daley, Nathan, and Taylor spotted him and waved back. Sensing his urgency, they began to run toward him. "We found somebody!" he shouted. "Technically, I found somebody because I was the—"

"Who is it?" Nathan asked breathlessly.

"Where did they come from?" Daley demanded.

"Are we rescued?" Taylor squealed.

Eric stopped running and had to bend over to catch his breath. "I don't know. I don't even know if they're alive."

The others stopped and looked somberly at

one another. They had been hoping all along that finding anyone else on the island would lead to getting rescued, and Eric hated to throw a wet blanket on their hopes. But he had to be honest—the person lying under the tree looked way beyond rescue.

It was finally Nathan who gritted his teeth and waved at the others to follow. They jogged determinedly back toward their starting point, and Eric had to scramble to keep up with them.

Nathan outpaced the others, and he had no difficulty following the muddy trail. *Somebody else is on the island, but that might not be the answer to our dilemma. It might just lead to more questions and bigger problems.*

He wished that Eric had more information, but what difference did it make? *We'll know soon enough*, he thought. *Even if we don't get rescued out of this, maybe we can help somebody else.*

With Eric pointing the way, Nathan continued to lead. He paused to shout, "Jackson!"

"Over here!" came the reply.

Nathan hurried toward the sound of voices, and he spotted another tree with a red ribbon tied to it. Under the tree, Nathan and Melissa were bent over a still figure, and all that attention made him hope that the person was still alive.

"They're over there!" He pointed the direction to Daley, Taylor, and Eric, then ran the rest of the way.

"Who is it?" Nathan asked, padding to a stop in the thick underbrush.

"It's Abby," Melissa answered gravely.

"Abby! Geez!" Nathan exclaimed, bending down to examine his friend. She looked so messed up. *Somebody should have stopped them from going. We should have stuck together.*

Daley and Eric caught up with them and gazed solemnly at their unconscious friend. Shock gave way to a flood of questions.

Daley asked, "Is she okay?"

"Does she look okay?" Jackson muttered.

Daley bent down and felt Abby's forehead. After a moment, she reported, "She's hot. She might have a fever."

Taylor finally caught up with the somber group, and she gazed with dismay at her classmate. "Whoa—Abby! She looks bad. And that's saying something, cause she is normally, like, gorgeous."

"We should get her back to camp," declared Daley.

Melissa nodded. "That's what I said."

Nathan leaned over his friend to study her injuries more closely. Not that he knew what he was looking at, but he wanted to help. "Is she okay to move?" he asked.

"I don't know," Daley answered, "but she's not okay to leave here." She turned to Melissa and said, "Run back to camp. Tell Lex to get the first-aid kit and take some of the drinking water down to the ocean to cool it off."

Melissa bristled at this order. "Well, why don't you—?"

"Then get some T-shirts," Daley said, paying no attention to her. "We can dip them in the water and use them to cool her down."

Nathan thought that Melissa was going to argue with this blunt order, but she turned away from Daley and looked at Abby. Seeing her friend in such bad shape, she nodded. "Fine."

After Melissa jogged off, Daley turned her attention to Taylor. "You should go with her."

"No, you go!" the blond girl protested.

Daley nodded sagely. "Okay, you stay here and help carry her back."

"Okay, I'll go," Taylor said quickly. She ran off before she lost sight of Melissa, and for once she ran fairly fast.

Nathan looked forlornly at his injured friend. "What happened to her? I don't know *who* I expected to find, but it wasn't Abby."

"You guys can do a crossover grip with your arms," Daley said. "Eric and I will relieve you."

"Yeah," Eric answered, who looked unusually somber as he gazed at Abby. "You know, I was almost going to go with them."

Jackson bent toward Nathan and extended his arms. "Are you up for this?"

He nodded. "Let's do it."

The boys formed a seat with their arms, and Daley and Eric helped to lift Abby. When they placed her in Nathan's arms, she felt oddly light and fragile, and he hoped they weren't making her injuries worse by moving her. But what else could they do? There were no stretchers or ambulances out here.

Melissa's mind was racing as she jogged through the forest. She was vaguely aware of Taylor stumbling along behind her, and she tried not to lose sight of her. Abby was one of her best friends, and it tore her apart to see her like that. She was smart and funny and everybody liked her, but none of that had helped her survive on this island.

I feel so helpless, Melissa thought. That was the real reason she was running back to camp, because she wanted to take charge of the first-aid kit. She knew the bag had smelling salts, aspirin, and other remedies that might help Abby, who suffered from exposure and dehydration, if nothing else.

I'm not going back because of Daley, she told herself. *I want to take care of Abby. It's that simple.*

Finally reaching the beach, she spotted Lex sitting atop the plane, working on the radio. He had apparently seen her first, because he waved.

"Lex! Lex!" she shouted, running out of breath. The boy dropped his tools, slid down the fuselage, and jumped off the wing. He ran out to meet her.

"It's Abby!" Melissa shouted. "She's unconscious and dehydrated. We have to—"

"I'll cool off some clean water," Lex said, running toward the fire pit. "You get T-shirts we can soak to cool her down!"

"Uh . . . yeah, right." Melissa bent over to catch her breath, wondering how a little kid knew so much. She took a few steps to get a better look at the clothesline, because she wanted clean cloths, if possible.

Heaving and panting, Taylor stumbled into camp. She saw Melissa and Lex heading in different directions, and she whined, "And I ran back here because—?"

Melissa didn't have time to deal with Taylor. Abby required all her attention. Summoning extra reserves of energy, she ran toward the clothesline, where several T's flapped in the salty breeze. She turned to Taylor and said, "Now it looks like that was a good idea to air out the sleeping bags. Abby will need the room."

"Yeah, I occasionally have a good idea," Taylor agreed. "But I don't know what to do for Abby."

"Help me then," Melissa answered. This was the time to take charge of the first-aid kit and make sure things were done correctly. Abby's life was at stake, and other lives might be, too. If they didn't bring her back to consciousness, they might never find out what happened to Jory, Ian, and the pilot.

Jackson brought up the rear of the rescue group, and he glanced nervously over his shoulder. Nathan was in front, while Eric and Daley struggled to carry the light but dead weight of the unconscious girl. He kept watch on the rocky forest around them, because they had no idea what dangers might be lurking there.

All he knew was something bad had happened to Abby, and three members of their crew were still missing. *Probably in big trouble.* The only thing clear at the moment was that Eric and Daley were eventually going to drop poor Abby.

Through clenched teeth, Eric rasped, "There's . . . got . . . to . . . be . . . a . . . better . . . way . . . to . . . do . . . this."

"Stop," Jackson ordered, unable to watch anymore. "Let's stop fooling around. Not in this terrain."

He rushed forward to catch the girl before Eric and Daley dropped her, and he draped Abby over his shoulder. Jackson felt the warmth of her fever and her beating heart against his skin. He took a few steps and knew this was going to go much faster than they could.

"I can do that, too," Nathan claimed.

"You'll get your chance," Jackson answered with a groan. Now he led the way, forcing all of them to make better time. He wanted to save Abby's life, but he also wanted to get out of the craggy woods and back to familiar territory.

Lex placed two big jugs of water in the surf to cool them down to ocean temperature. Their drinking water was pretty warm from boiling and then sitting in the sun all day, but it was all they had to cool down a fever. Melissa collected T-shirts and other light cotton garments, while Taylor was supposed to be gathering sleeping bags. Mostly she seemed to be admiring her new necklace.

Since the crash, Lex had spent every moment trying to figure out how to get them rescued. From the signal kite to the radio to the SOS raft, he had tried everything. The others had helped, but none of them really thought all of his efforts were necessary. They had placed a lot of faith in Captain Russell's being able to find help on the island.

That hope was dashed now.

"Get the water!" a voice shouted, and he turned to see Daley charge into camp ahead of the others.

Taylor jumped to her feet. "Hey! They're back!"

Lex grabbed the water jugs from the foamy surf and rushed to the fire pit. That was where Melissa was spreading the cleanest of their sleeping bags under the shade of the canopy. Nathan came staggering in with Abby draped across his back and Jackson and Eric right behind him.

"Put her over here!" Melissa shouted. She smoothed out a sleeping bag and put T-shirts into the nose cone they used as a washbasin.

"This is as cool as it gets," Lex said, lugging the cold water to the fire pit.

Jackson took the containers from Lex, and Taylor actually grabbed two more and hustled them down to the beach. Gently they laid Abby onto the bed they'd made, and Lex squeezed through the crowd to get a look at her. She looked beaten up, but she wasn't seriously injured from what he could see.

They poured water, wet the T-shirts, and plied Abby's head with cool rags. Daley squeezed a bit of moisture onto her lips. "Even if she can't swallow, some of this has got to find its way in," she said.

"Not too much," Melissa cautioned. "She might choke."

From the look the two girls exchanged, Lex figured out that their feud was still going on, but they were going to bury it to take care of Abby.

"Let's swap out the rags," Melissa said. "We

gotta keep her cool." She touched her skin and frowned. "Her sunburn is really bad. Do we still have that ointment?"

"The one I'm allergic to?" Daley asked. "Or the stuff in the blue tube?"

"Blue tube," Melissa answered.

"I'll get it," Jackson said, rushing toward the plane.

"There are some straws in the cabin!" yelled Nathan. "We could use, like . . . a drip system to make her drink."

"Good idea!" Jackson answered, who was already halfway to the plane.

Lex leaned forward and said, "There's aspirin in the first-aid kit. I could mix some in water."

"Good, go!" Daley answered.

"I'll get salt tablets, too!" Lex said.

"How does he know so much?" Eric asked.

When Lex returned with a coconut bowl, a hammer, and the pills he needed, they were putting cool cloths on Abby's neck and shoulders. Drop by drop, Daley managed to get some water into the injured girl's mouth, and Lex thought he saw her swallow.

Melissa touched her head and seemed satisfied that she was cooler. "I think we should keep her in the shade until the sun goes down," she said.

Daley nodded in agreement. "Yeah, then we can move her into our tent."

"What can we do?" Nathan asked.

"We're gonna need a lot more cool water to get her body temperature down," Melissa answered. "We may need to boil more water, too. We're using it awfully fast."

"Water duty," Eric said. "I know about that." He grabbed two empty jugs and headed down the path to the well.

"I'll build up the fire," Nathan said.

Lex ground up aspirin and salt pills and mixed them with a little water. Daley took a straw, cut it in half, and was able to give Abby the liquid drop by drop. Melissa watched with a look of approval on her face, but Lex knew what she was thinking.

We're all busy, all doing what we can, but will any of it work?

Taylor brought more cool water from the ocean, and she stopped to take a worried look at Abby. "Is she going to be okay?" the blond girl asked.

Melissa and Daley glanced at each other, but neither one of them had an answer.

TEN

As twilight fell and the temperatures cooled, they moved Abby into the freshly cleaned girls' tent. Daley and Melissa tended to her, as they had been doing, while the others gathered around the campfire. This was their traditional dinnertime, and Jackson had cut up the fruit Nathan and Eric had collected earlier.

That seems like days ago, Nathan thought, *not just this morning*.

He wasn't very hungry, and nobody else ate much, either. The rest of them were lost in grim thought, and the only one who kept busy was Lex, tuning his radio. All day he scanned the frequencies and announced their presence, getting every kind of static known to man or space aliens. But no rescuers.

Eric nibbled at a banana that he normally would have wolfed down. He sighed and remarked, "I never thought something truly bad was going to happen to any of us . . . until now."

The others nodded somberly, except for Taylor, who looked angry. "What about Jory? And Ian?" she demanded. "And the pilot person? Why weren't they together?"

Nathan shook his head. "They've gotta turn up sooner or later."

"Unless they're in worse shape than Abby," Eric muttered.

"You guys are such downers," Taylor complained. "I know we're going to be rescued . . . and soon!" Wearing a pout, she threw up her hands and marched off toward the surf, where she had more water bottles cooling.

That left the three older boys alone together, and Nathan asked a question that had been nagging him all day. "Do you think we ought to set watches?"

"Why do we need watches?" Eric scoffed. "We don't have to be anywhere at any certain time."

"Not those kind of watches," Nathan answered glumly. "The kind where somebody stays up at night and . . . watches. So far we've been jumping into our sleeping bags and sleeping, but we could take turns staying awake."

Jackson frowned in thought and poked at the fire with a stick. "You think we could have a visitor in the middle of the night?"

Nathan shrugged. "Well, we don't know what happened to Abby and the others, do we? We have no idea what's beyond the small area we've explored. Captain Russell or Ian or Jory might stumble into camp, too. Somebody should be awake."

"I'll take first watch," Eric said bravely. "I knew all those daytime naps would come in handy."

Jackson finally nodded in agreement. "Okay. I've been thinking about staying up at night, too, but for a different reason. What if a ship passed by in the night? Or a plane? We'd never know it if we're all asleep."

"Yeah, and we could probably spot their lights from far off," Nathan said excitedly.

"And we still have a few flares left," Eric added, giving Nathan a sly smile. "They work best at night, right?"

Nathan lowered his head, because he had wasted one of their flares, along with the signal kite. There was no way to bring them back, but he could start being more responsible right now. After what happened to Abby—whatever it was— it was more important than ever to get rescued. And to stay alert.

"I'll take middle watch," Nathan said. "So, Eric, you wake me up about one o'clock. Jackson, I'll wake you up about three thirty, and you're on duty until everyone else wakes up."

"I hope 'everyone' includes Abby," Eric replied. He slapped his head. "Oh, now I *do* have to set my watch. Well, it's a small price to pay for protecting the camp."

"Check with Lex," Nathan said. "He has the correct time."

Eric shrugged. "Of course he does. He knows everything."

The boys were quiet for a while, until they saw Taylor leave the tent and head their way, carrying a bundle of soiled T-shirts. "Don't tell the girls about this," Jackson said. "I don't want to worry them."

"Yeah, they have enough to worry about," Nathan answered. "Like getting Abby well."

Melissa followed Taylor out of the tent when she took the dirty linen away. But she didn't follow her to the fire pit, even though she knew there was food waiting. Daley sat on a nearby log, and Melissa sat beside her on the cooler. They were both wiped out from all the effort they had expended. If there was any way to *will* Abby awake, then she should be awake.

Daley wrung a cloth in her hands, looking as though she were wringing a chicken's neck—she was so frustrated. Melissa stayed by her side, and they both gazed at the sunset for a while. It could be so peaceful and serene here, thought Melissa, but that was an illusion when danger lurked so near.

She pointed to the distant fire pit. "Taylor says they have dinner going."

"Yeah, I know."

"What else can we do?" Mel asked.

Daley heaved her shoulders. "I think we've done all we can."

Melissa could feel herself near tears, or screaming, or both. She knew Daley wasn't far behind. "This whole trip," she said in a raspy voice, "has been a bad dream that keeps getting worse."

Daley sniffed and her voice trembled when she said, "We've done our best and . . . whatever happens, remember that."

All the tears and emotions, good and bad, spilled out, and the two friends clung to each other in a desperate hug. The girls cried until their throats were parched, and it felt good not to cry alone.

When Melissa finally pulled away, she said, "I wish I had your confidence."

Daley looked embarrassed. "Hey, look, I know sometimes I can be a little . . . overbearing."

Melissa smiled, and she wanted to say, "Sometimes?" But none of them could help being the people they were.

Daley went on, "You're such a totally sane, selfless person, and I'm sorry about what I said. Please don't change."

"Thank you," Melissa rasped. "I'm sorry, too."

"Daley?" a feminine voice called.

"We're over here, Taylor," she answered, but she kept her eyes on Melissa. "You know what, you found the necklace—you should keep it."

Melissa gave a surprised laugh. "What necklace?"

"Really?" Daley said with a smile.

"Daley?" came the call.

"Over here, Taylor!"

Melissa made a dismissive wave. "Oh, let's just give it to Taylor. It's more her style anyway."

"Perfect!" Daley held out her hand, and they shook to seal the deal.

"Daley!"

"That didn't sound like Taylor," Melissa said with a frown. She glanced at the fire pit, where Taylor was talking to the boys, then turned slowly toward the tent. Daley blinked at her, and both of them jumped to their feet and dashed inside.

When they stumbled into the tent, mouths agape, Abby lifted her head and smiled weakly. "Could I have some water?" she asked.

Melissa sank to her knees, overcome with a sense of relief. She almost cried and hugged Abby, but her friend was still too weak for that. Daley pumped her fist in triumph, dove for the bottle, and handed it to Abby. With all that sunburned and bruised skin, her friend looked like a peeled mango, but she was alive and drinking. Drinking too fast.

"Take it easy," Daley said, gently grabbing the bottle. "Drink slow. We don't want you choking now."

Melissa just kept on grinning. "You're dehydrated, but you're going to be okay."

Abby looked around at the dingy tent and asked, "Where am I?"

"You just joined Club Twenty-Nine Down," Daley answered. "Welcome to the party!"

Daley stepped out of the tent and yelled at the top of her lungs, "Abby is awake! She's okay!"

A few seconds later, Daley was surrounded by chattering and concerned people, peppering her with questions. "How is she? What happened? Where are the others? Did they find anything? Are we rescued?"

"No, we're not rescued yet," she told Taylor. Then Daley lowered her voice to add, "Listen, she's still really weak. Let's give her time to adjust. Don't get in her face, okay?"

They nodded their heads in agreement, but only Jackson took a step back.

"Sure, we'll go easy on her," Nathan promised.

"Of course," Taylor said.

"Does she know I saved her life?" Eric asked.

The tent flap opened, and Abby shuffled out, leaning on Melissa for support. She managed a wan smile until half the crowd lunged at her. "Abby! What happened? Where's everybody else?" they demanded. "Where did you go? Is there civilization out there? Did someone attack you?"

Daley rolled her eyes, and she could see Jackson shaking his head at the outburst. It would have been funny, but the dazed expression on Abby's face wasn't funny. She was still unsteady on her feet, so Melissa took her to one of the airplane seats anchored in the sand.

Gently, Daley pushed the others back. "C'mon. Let her breathe," she ordered. "If you'll be quiet, maybe she'll answer you."

They finally settled down, and a hush fell over the group of young survivors. The darkening sky was dotted with a thousand stars and another thousand blossoming every second. At a distance, the fire popped and sizzled, and the ocean lapped the shore.

Abby seemed to take a moment to look at each one of them in turn, and Daley wondered how much she really remembered. "Thanks, everyone," she said with a weak smile. Everyone smiled back, especially the boys, and she went on. "I didn't think I was going to make it."

"Yeah, neither did we," Eric said, for which Daley gave him a boot in the shin. "Ow."

For a moment, Abby looked like a foreigner who doesn't quite understand the language. When her gaze landed on Taylor, she got a big grin. Taylor smiled back, looking happy over the attention.

"Hey! You found it!" exclaimed Abby.

Taylor frowned in thought and looked down at her cute sundress. "Found what?"

"My necklace." Abby pointed to Taylor's neck. "I took it off before the crash. I was afraid I might choke or something. I never thought I'd see it again."

Daley looked at Melissa and nodded, because that was a fitting end to their materialism. Heck, they would trade all their jewelry for a chance to call home and tell their families they were all right.

Reluctantly, Taylor took off the gorgeous necklace and handed it over to its rightful owner. "We were keeping it safe for you," she said with a forced smile.

"Thank you." Abby clutched the necklace as though it was the most important thing in the world, and she seemed content for a moment.

Nathan leaned forward and asked, "Abby, what happened? Where's everybody else?"

An expression of horror passed over Abby's face, and her eyes widened in alarm. She turned away from them, as if she couldn't face her friends or anyone else. "You're not gonna believe what I've been through," she murmured.

When she didn't say anything else, Melissa prodded her. "What did you find out there?"

She rubbed her head and looked distracted. "It was like . . . like . . . I don't think I can find the right words."

"Try!" urged Taylor.

Abby rose unsteadily to her feet and stared off into the distance. Before she could answer, she stumbled, and Eric and Jackson caught her. Carefully, they eased her back onto her seat.

"I'm . . . I'm still so dizzy," she said in apology.

"Let's get her back in the tent," suggested Jackson. "I think she should rest some more." He didn't wait for anyone to help him as he guided the dazed girl back to her sleeping bag.

Taylor flapped her arms in frustration. "But I want to know what happened!"

Jackson came out and said, "It can wait."

"This is so unfair!" Taylor complained. She stepped between Daley and Melissa and got a concerned look on her face. "Um, whose sleeping bag is she using?"

Daley winced. "Oh, I forgot. Yours."

"No way!" Taylor answered. "Why can't she use Melissa's?"

"Why mine?" the dark-haired girl asked. "Don't be so selfish."

"And she'll need clothes, too," Daley said.

Now Taylor's eyes widened in horror. "Don't even go there."

"You have more clothes than anyone!" Daley protested.

"And I need them all!" Taylor glared at Melissa and said, "She still owes me a shirt."

"No, I don't."

"Yes, you do. And Daley is more her size."

"I am not."

"Don't give away my stuff!" Taylor insisted.

Daley scowled. "Whose stuff should we give her?"

"The boys' clothes."

Melissa scoffed. "Boys' clothes? I don't see you wearing boys' clothes."

"Why don't we flip a coin?" Daley asked.

"I'm not playing!" Taylor cried.

Suddenly, Abby stuck her head out of the tent and smiled gratefully at the three girls. "Hey, guys," she said. "Thanks."

Instantly, they were all smiles and sympathy. "It's okay. No problem," Taylor said.

"You'd do the same for us," Melissa added.

"It's all taken care of," Daley assured her.

As soon as Abby went back into the tent, the squabbling resumed. "My stuff is *my* stuff. Give away *your* stuff."

"You are so selfish!"

While they argued, Eric stepped up to Jackson and said, "And a new player enters the game. This is gonna be fun."

Jackson frowned worriedly and gazed at the shorter teen. "What do you think about Abby?"

"She's hot."

"No," Jackson whispered. "How is she acting? I don't know her very well."

Eric stroked his chin and said, "Well, she used

to get straight A's, but I don't think she could pass study hall at the moment."

"Yeah," Jackson agreed, nodding his head grimly.

A voice behind him piped in, "I think she's suffering from shock and maybe a little amnesia."

Jackson whirled around and looked down to see Lex. Darkness was falling quickly, and the ten-year-old had sneaked up on them.

"But she knows who she is," Eric scoffed.

The kid shrugged. "There are different kinds of amnesia. It's not always total amnesia like in the movies."

"How do you know so much?" Eric asked suspiciously.

"Forget that now," Jackson said with a scowl. "We'll find out what happened to her when we find out. About tonight . . ." He caught himself and looked down at Lex. "Um, don't you have, like, a radio to fix? "

The kid narrowed his eyes at them. "I know you guys are up to something—I just hope it won't be something stupid."

"How would you ever guess that?" Eric asked nervously.

Jackson shrugged his shoulders and looked around. They were alone in the long shadows of twilight, and the fading sun had turned the clouds a vibrant shade of pinkish-purple mixed with gold. Lex might be useful on night watch, and for sure he would be a pain if they didn't tell him.

"Okay," Jackson whispered, "we're keeping watches tonight. Someone will be on guard duty until dawn. We didn't tell the girls, because they need to sleep and take care of Abby. Three of us, so three shifts."

"I can do one, too!" Lex said eagerly.

Eric smiled at the kid and draped his arm over his scrawny shoulders. "Hey, little buddy, why don't you help me do my watch? We'll go to bed after we wake Nathan up about one a.m. Think of it as a slumber party!"

Lex looked up at Jackson and grinned, and then Jackson couldn't tell him no. Heck, the kid would probably do most of the work on a shift with Eric. "Okay," said their leader with a nod.

"What do you want us to do?" Lex asked excitedly.

Jackson surveyed the last bronze rays of the sun vanishing behind the swaying palm trees, and his paranoia suddenly felt a little silly. Then again, rescue could come at night just as easily as during the day. So could trouble.

"Watch for ships," he answered. "Do your radio thing. Watch for people straggling into camp. If Abby found her way back, maybe the others will, too."

"Watch for the bogeyman," Eric whispered into Lex's ear.

"None of that," Jackson growled. "And no practical jokes—this is serious business. And if you wake me up to report an intruder, it had better be the real thing."

Eric and Lex nodded somberly, and Jackson pointed to the fire pit. "If there's any trouble, the butcher knife is in the stump."

Eric gulped and nodded his head. "Okay, chief."

ELEVEN

The girls' tent went dark—as dark as the moonless night all around them—and Eric squirmed in his seat by the campfire. A piece of damp driftwood popped in the flames, making him jump. "Stupid wood," he muttered.

A few minutes later, the boys' tent went dark, too. Eric looked around, wondering where his assistant was. Then he heard the familiar static, and he knew Lex was messing with his radio. The only other sounds were the squawk of a night bird and the constant churning of the waves.

Eric turned and watched the jungle for a while, but no one came out of it. He watched the ocean, but he saw no lights of passing ships. Just the blackness that seemed to stretch on forever. Even the stars were socked in by low clouds that warned of coming rain. Both ends of the beach were quiet, except for the static from Lex's radio.

Eric yawned. "If you think this island is boring during the day," he said aloud, "you ought to see it at night."

He checked his watch, which he was wearing for the first time since the crash, and saw that it was only ten thirty. *Still two and a half hours to go before I can wake up Nathan to relieve me. Wasn't this guard duty Nathan's idea? Maybe he should do an extra shift?*

Jugs of dirty water from the well were waiting to be boiled and filtered, but that was too much like real work. Eric had a functioning flashlight, thanks to their solar battery charger, and he tried to make some shadow puppets. They looked like blobby monsters in the sand, so he stopped being creative.

"Whatcha doing?" asked a voice that made him jump.

Eric turned to see Lex grinning at him.

"I'm trying to stay awake," he answered. "But since you're here, I don't have to worry about that anymore. The butcher knife is in the stump." He stretched out on a beach towel and lowered his hat over his eyes.

"Wait a minute," Lex said with concern. "We're on guard duty. I think that means staying awake."

"I'm giving you what you wanted, which is a shift of your own. Thank me in the morning. And don't forget to wake up Nathan at one o'clock."

Eric yawned and closed his eyes.

The kid sat beside him on one of the airplane seats. "I'll talk to you to keep you awake," he said. "Want me to show you how to work the radio?"

Eric groaned. "I don't need lessons to pick up static. Why don't you take the flashlight and find some more firewood? This stuff is wet."

"Out in the dark?" the kid asked. "Did I ever tell you about this great science fair project I did last year? I took getting electricity out of a potato to a new place! I wanted to show which kinds of potatoes generated the most current, and I used a crystal radio as the benchmark."

Eric would have rolled his eyes if they weren't closed. As it was, he was able to doze a bit as Lex rambled on about potatoes and radios. Every now and then, Eric said, "Uh-huh."

Suddenly, his companion attacked him, shaking his shoulder violently. "Wake up!" he whispered urgently.

"What?" Eric muttered, not sure where he was. "I was studying, Ms. Norris—I wasn't asleep."

"This isn't school," Lex whispered. "There's something moving around in the bushes."

"Huh?" Eric sat up and looked around at the oppressive darkness. He had never seen their little beach community so dead and lifeless before—it was as if even the birds and the fish were asleep. Because of that stillness, he clearly heard the rustling beyond the trees.

Eric jumped to his feet and backed away from the shadowy bushes. "What time is it?"

Lex shined the flashlight onto his watch. "Just before midnight."

"Ssshh!" Eric put his fingers to his lips, and they both listened intently. A sawing sound mixed in with the breaking waves to form an uneasy rhythm, and Eric craned his neck to find the direction.

His eyes focused on the tents, and he laughed. "That's just Jackson snoring."

"W-Well, what was in the bushes?" Lex demanded.

Eric peered into the overgrown darkness but couldn't see anything beyond the first line of trees and ferns. "Give me the flashlight."

"Shouldn't we go wake up Jackson?" Lex asked.

"To say what? That we heard a leaf move?" Eric grabbed the flashlight and pointed the beam into the thick foliage, where it got swallowed up in a black hole of jungle rot. A big fern waved at him, making him jump back, and he heard scuffling sounds.

"Is everybody in a tent?" Eric asked suspiciously. "Let's make sure they're not punkin' us."

"I checked a little while ago," Lex answered, "and they were."

Eric stiffened his spine and reached for the

long kitchen knife stuck in the stump. His hand trembled as he tried to level the wavering beam at the moving greenery. "Let's give them a surprise and go after them," he said, sticking out his chin. "You go first."

"Me?" Lex asked in amazement. "You have the knife and the flashlight."

"So I got you covered," Eric answered, hefting his weapon.

The ten-year-old shook his head and stepped bravely down the path. Eric followed him, sweeping the beam over as big an area as he could, but nothing looked amiss. A sweet-smelling breeze grazed Eric's face, making him feel as though he was being a wuss.

"You know, there are rats in these palm trees," Lex said. "That could be what we heard."

"Rats?" echoed Eric with a scowl. "Then why are we eating seaweed?"

He cast the flashlight beam all around the towering trees and lush plants and finally shrugged his shoulders. "There's nothing here."

That's when a log dropped into the fire, and a plume of sparks shot into the night air, startling both boys. Eric whirled around to see a shadow dart from the fire pit and vanish into the deep shadows of the wrecked plane. He cast his light in that direction, but he was too slow to spot anything.

"Who was *that*?" Eric asked nervously.

"Who?" Lex said. "I didn't see anyone."

Eric shook his head in frustration. "Kid, you started this whole thing. Now you say it's just tree rats?"

"Sorry...I got scared," Lex said with a sheepish smile. "I need to get back to my radio."

Still shaking his head, Eric led the way out of the forest back to the fire pit. Once again, he reclined on his beach towel and pulled his hat over his head. "Okay, now I deserve a nap. Don't wake me up until it's one o'clock."

"Okay," Lex promised.

Within a few minutes, Eric was transported back to a happy, simpler time when his biggest worry was getting big laughs in biology. His dream was like a highlight film of his biggest antics, and he didn't even mind going to detention. For some reason, Taylor was in detention hall—along with Jackson. That Jackson butted in on everything.

Eric's former reality and his surreal present blended together to make a very potent dream world. Taylor agreed to go with him to the prom, where they danced under swaying palm trees and a clothesline filled with dirty sleeping bags. Soon he was kissing Taylor, and she was nuzzling his neck and slobbering on his cheek.

She snorted in his ear, and he said, "Oh, baby."

Then his dream took an abrupt turn for the worst. Taylor was kissing Jackson, and he was in an airplane crash and got stranded on an island. "Eric, wake up," whispered an annoying voice that wasn't Taylor anymore.

"Whaa . . . " Eric blinked awake to find Lex gripping his shirt and looking around nervously. Eric's cheek felt cool, and he touched his skin to find it wet and gooey. "Were you kissing me?" demanded Eric.

"No!" The kid looked at him as if he were crazy. "You were dreaming."

Eric held out his damp hand. "Why is there slobber on my cheek?"

"I don't know, but there's *somebody* in the plane." Lex pointed worriedly behind him. "They're moving around, looking for something."

Eric staggered to his feet and brushed the sand off his pants. He paused to listen to the night, and he did hear faint crashing and bumping sounds coming from the wrecked DeHavilland. At the other end of camp, the sleeping tents remained quiet.

"You were sitting there," Eric whispered. "How did you let somebody get past you?"

"I was soldering," Lex explained. "It takes lots of concentration to solder."

Eric rubbed his face with exasperation and felt more mystery slobber. Shaking his head, he walked slowly toward the airplane, which was eerily lit by Lex's battery-operated work light.

"Is everybody else still asleep?" Eric asked.

"Yes. We don't wake up Nathan for half an hour."

Eric frowned at the brat. "Let's not wake up anyone until we find out if this is your imagination . . . again."

Unfortunately, the closer he got to the dented hulk, the louder the noises became. It was clear that someone was inside the plane, rummaging through their supplies. *Crash! Bang! Thump!* Whoever it was was trashing all their stuff.

"Give me the knife," he whispered to Lex.

The kid shrugged. "I don't have the knife—I thought *you* had the knife."

Eric muttered something under his breath, then he tried to make his voice sound like Jackson's— deep and dumb. "Okay, who's in there?" he barked.

The noises abruptly stopped, and both Eric and Lex froze. Something black and hairy smashed against one of the windows, causing the boys to leap backward and stumble in the sand. A second later, the sounds from the plane were back to minor thuds and bumps, just as it had been when they first approached.

Eric gulped and staggered to his feet. "Okay, now I'm gonna wake up Jackson," he whispered. "You stay here and watch 'em."

"Me?" Lex asked. "You want to leave the little kid alone with the intruder?"

Eric scowled and pointed to the tent. "All right, you go wake them up."

Lex didn't need to be told twice as he darted off to fetch help. That was when the bangs and thuds began a clear path toward the open door, and Eric realized that the burglar was trying to get out. He couldn't run—he had to stay and at least get a look at their mystery intruder.

I have to find something to use as a shield, Eric thought. He picked up a broken door panel just as something black and hairy darted across the doorway, running on four legs. Eric threw his shield against the opening to block its escape, and he felt two strong collisions as the animal tried to break out. With a loud snort, the beast scampered to the back of the dark cabin, and Eric let out his breath.

Everything was quiet by the time Lex arrived with drowsy Jackson and Nathan stumbling behind him. "The intruder is right in here," Lex said, pointing to the plane.

The four boys stood perfectly still and listened ... but there was nothing to hear, because the sneaky burglar was hiding. Jackson yawned and grumbled, "What did I tell you guys about yanking our chain?"

"It tried to escape a second ago!" exclaimed Eric, jumping to his feet. "I battled it! I kept it from getting away! It was big and hairy, and it kissed me ..."

Jackson waved his finger at Eric. "If you expect me to fall for this ..."

Lex tugged on the big guy's shirtsleeve and said, "Jackson, I heard it first. There *was* something in the plane. Really."

"It's still in there," Eric insisted.

"Well, go in and get it," Nathan said, "or apologize for waking us up." He tossed the flashlight to Eric, who fumbled the catch but finally held onto the torch.

He gulped and stepped into the doorway. "I'll lead the way, but I won't go alone."

Muttering and grumbling, Jackson and Nathan lined up behind him, while Lex stayed outside. Slowly the three boys entered the dark recesses of the wrecked plane, and Eric shined the light around. They had removed most of the seats, but the cabin was still a repository for supplies and assorted junk. Several of the boxes had been tipped over, and there was broken glass in the aisle.

"You made a mess," Jackson said. "Were you sleeping in here?"

"No!" Eric answered. "I tell you there's an intruder!" He stomped to the back of the cabin, kicking the boxes and yelling and hooting. "Come out, come out, wherever you are!"

Suddenly, a creature broke from the shadows and scurried between Eric's legs, causing him to jump and throw the flashlight into the air. When it smashed to the floor, the cabin was plunged into darkness, and Jackson and Nathan crashed into each other. All three boys lunged for the fleeing figure as it scampered around the cabin, but it eluded them in the darkness.

The boys thrashed around, trying to corral the mystery beast, until Lex stuck his head into the door. "Too late," he said. "I saw it run away."

Eric dragged himself to his feet. "What was it?"

Before he could answer, Daley stuck her head in the doorway. "What are you guys doing?" she hissed. "Do you want to wake up Abby?"

All three of them stammered at once, and she just shook her head. "Goofy boys. Keep it quiet, or there won't be any breakfast for *any* of you." Daley stomped away, leaving them all chagrined.

Jackson sat up and rubbed his head. "Okay, does anybody know what happened?"

"Uh, I think I know what it was," answered Nathan. He crawled out of the wrecked plane and checked the tracks in the sand. Finally he laughed and said, "I can't believe it. Not the pig!"

"What pig?" Eric asked.

Nathan looked embarrassed. "The wild pig Daley and I caught. Uh, we had to let it go."

"You didn't tell us you caught a pig," Eric said accusingly. "Did you ever hear of a ham sandwich? That would be good about now."

"Yeah, I know," Nathan muttered. "Sorry, but I couldn't cut its throat, and neither could Daley."

Lex shook his head and laughed. "Eric, you said that something kissed you. It must've been the pig!"

Eric gaped at them and touched his cheek.

"So, Eric, how was it?" Nathan asked playfully.

Jackson smiled. "I hear once you've been kissed by a pig, you never go back to girls."

"And I thought the pig liked *me*," Nathan said in shock.

"Okay, okay," Eric muttered, throwing up his hands and walking away. "Ask me if I'll ever do night guard duty again."

"Eric, will you—"

"No!" he shouted.

TWELVE

he next morning, Daley made sure that Abby got something to eat and drink, and she insisted that her patient continue to rest. All the others went back to their regular chores, having not done much work the day before. Melissa and Eric were on water detail, Lex was working on the radio, and Nathan and Jackson were building a new canopy over the fire pit. This one would be made of bamboo with a thatched palm roof.

Taylor was . . . well, she was charging batteries.

Daley looked around and found that no one was watching her. So she turned on the video camera and began her diary.

Daley

It's been over a week since we crashed. On day one, the pilot and three of our friends hiked off to explore the island. One of them came back. Alone. We still don't know what happened to them. I'm not even sure that Abby remembers all of it. We're on edge about this, but we've got a routine now. That's helping us get along. One thing is for sure, it's good to have Abby back.

Eric's video diary was much different.

Eric

If I didn't find Abby out in the jungle, she wouldn't have made it. The word "hero" is so overused, but not here. I'm a hero.

It was rare for Lex to add to his video diary, but he took some time to leave his thoughts.

Lex

We're all worried about rescue. But since we can't do much about that, we spend most of our time doing basic survival stuff. After a week or so, I think we finally learned how to live with one another, and work together.

Something caught his eye in camp, and he noticed that Abby had left the girls' tent and was being sociable.

We should be okay for a while, as long as nothing new happens to mess things up.

This morning can't start out any worse, Taylor thought as she balanced an untied bundle of bamboo stalks in her arms. She had been efficiently charging batteries with the solar panel when Jackson had grabbed her for this duty. Hauling bamboo? Why did the fire pit need a new canopy? Sure, the old one occasionally blew away, but it still kept rain off the fire. Mostly.

Meanwhile, her Highness gets to sleep in and do nothing! Sure, Abby is blistered, bruised, and sunburned, but aren't we all? I still hold the prize for Most Horrible Blisters from digging that latrine. Plus she's using my sleeping bag!

Taylor tried to put that out of her mind, because Abby did need their help. This island wasn't a vacation paradise, despite its looking like a TV commercial.

If I just didn't have to balance all these bamboo sticks, I'd be happy! Suddenly, the stalks shifted in every wrong direction at once, and Taylor gasped in panic. She juggled them unsuccessfully for a moment until they all tumbled out of her arms and clattered to the ground.

"Oh, shoot!" Taylor pouted and stamped her foot.

"Can I help?" a pleasant voice asked.

Taylor whirled around to see Abby smiling sweetly at her. "Sure," the blond girl snapped. "Make a boat and get me out of here. That would help."

Abby just kept smiling, and that's when Taylor noticed her red print top and khaki shorts— hanging on Abby's perfect bones.

She wagged her finger. "Um . . . is this a sick dream or is that my top? And shorts?"

Abby shrugged apologetically. "I lost my gear in the jungle. I didn't think you'd mind."

"Oh, you didn't?" Taylor squeaked, barely controlling her rage. "Well let me tell you something—"

Abby bent down to pick up the fallen bamboo. "I'm sorry, Taylor," she said sweetly. "Let me do this for you."

"Let me be clear," Taylor murmured. "If you think you're gonna waltz in here and—" She was about to bawl Abby out when she realized that the new arrival was doing her work for her. Abby was a big strong girl with long arms, and carrying the bamboo was no problem for her.

"Yeah," Taylor cooed. "Maybe you should do that for me. Take it right over there to the fire pit."

Taylor

Okay, so she lost all her stuff and doesn't have any clothes and almost, like, died. Welcome to paradise! But if she wants to wear *my* clothes, she's gonna have to do my chores. That's the law. You can look it up.

The whole beach smelled fresher this morning, thought Nathan, as if someone had given it a bath in perfume. The sun was brighter, the waves foamier, and the breezes swirled through the palm fronds, coming out of the jungle. That always brought a flowery scent, but it was even stronger this morning. The ocean was a transparent turquoise color that he had never seen before. It glistened like an immense jewel.

Maybe it was seeing Abby walking around camp, talking to everyone, that brightened the day. After what she had been through, it was amazing to see her so happy and healthy. Then again, what *had* Abby been through? They still didn't know.

"Are you ready?" Jackson asked, bringing Nathan's mind back from the clouds.

"Yeah," he answered. Nathan got a good grip on the vine rope and nodded. "Let's do it."

"One . . . two . . . three . . . pull!" Jackson said.

With each one of them yanking on a rope tied to a corner pole, Jackson and Nathan labored in unison to erect the frame for the new canopy. Like magic, the four poles stood straight up and swayed for a moment, but they stayed upright.

"Yeah!" Nathan shouted. The two boys gave each other high fives, because that was the hardest part. Now all they had to do was tie palm fronds to the top and lash the rest of the bamboo to the frame to give the structure stability. Then the new canopy would be ready to protect their precious fire.

Nathan looked around, wondering what was taking Taylor so long. Where was the rest of their bamboo? That's when he saw Abby, carrying the long stalks in her arms.

She stopped to admire their creation. "Wow! That's really great!"

"Abby!" Nathan said. He ran toward her and grabbed the poles. "Don't carry that stuff!"

"Thanks." She flashed him a brilliant smile that reminded him why she had been one of the most popular girls in school. Abby was one of the good people . . . and the gorgeous people.

"How are you feeling?" Jackson asked with concern.

"Fine." Despite her scratches and sunburn, Abby did look a lot better, almost back to normal. Tons of water, some gentle care, and a good night's sleep had worked wonders for her.

"Is there any food left?" she asked politely.

"I'll get you something," Jackson promised. He dropped all his tools and the rope and hurried toward the plane. Nathan looked curiously after him, because it wasn't like Jackson to play nurse. True, they were all worried about Abby and wanted to take care of her, but Jackson hardly knew her. *Special care from Jackson*, he wondered. *What does that mean?*

Abby kept smiling at him, as if she was just glad to be alive. "Sit," Nathan ordered. "You're forbidden to do anything until you're better."

He conducted her to a seat by the fire, even though it was a glorious, sunny day. Abby touched his hand and said, "It's okay, I'm fine."

"I know, but let's be sure." Nathan sat down beside her and waited to see what she would say. He was determined not to bug her for information.

She pointed to the half-built canopy. "That's very cool."

"Thanks. It's to keep rain off the fire."

Abby nodded, looking impressed. "You guys are doing really well."

"We're trying," Nathan said with a shrug. "Not like we have a lot of choice."

On that somber note, Abby's smile faded. "So ...
the others ... they haven't come back?" she asked
softly.

"No," he admitted. "We were kinda hoping
you could tell us what happened to them."

Now her smile faded completely, and she
gazed into the flames of the fire, lost in some kind
of inner turmoil. Nathan didn't know what to say,
and he wished he could take his question back.
It was as though Abby was suffering from battle
fatigue—she had seen and done too much in the
last week.

Nathan had lived a regular life before this,
and he had never dealt with anyone who was
traumatized. "I'll get you a cup of water," he said.

She smiled gratefully. "I would like that."

Everyone else seemed to be working on a
pet project today—the boys on the canopy, Lex
on the radio, Daley pounding seaweed into green
jelly. So Melissa picked today to finish her pet
project. She had carved several coconut husks
into cute little half-cups, but they weren't going
to use them for drinking. What they needed most
around camp was light, without wasting battery
power.

Last night, there had been a commotion, and
nobody could see anything. Daley had checked

it out and said it was just the boys, acting silly, but it demonstrated how much they needed more light.

Proudly, Melissa finished her first prototype and set it on Lex's workbench. He was working atop the plane, tuning in every frequency he could find, and she didn't want to bother him. Movement caught her eye, and she saw Jackson jogging her way. That brought a hopeful smile to Melissa's face, as she wondered if he was coming over to see her.

He gave her a nod as he rushed toward the food containers. He opened one and began filling his arms with leftovers.

Melissa held up her prototype and said, "Hey, look! A little oil from the plane, a strip of cloth, and ta-da! Candles."

Jackson was so busy collecting food that he barely noticed her, and he didn't respond. "Is it lunchtime already?" she asked pleasantly.

He nodded enthusiastically. "For Abby. She's up and looks a *whole* lot better."

"Excellent!" Melissa held up her invention again. "What do you think of my . . ."

Without a word, Jackson hurried off, carrying most of the food they had in stock. Melissa gave him a bemused smile and looked at her homemade candle. Well, maybe it didn't compare with Abby coming back from the dead, but it was still going to be useful.

That's not fair to Jackson, she chided herself. *He's only trying to be helpful.*

Melissa stopped to make an entry in her video diary.

Melissa

I'm so glad Abby's okay. I always liked her. She's smart and cute and fun. So smart and cute and...

Cute.

Melissa frowned and turned off the camera. She set down her candle, jumped to her feet, and followed Jackson back to the fire pit.

When she got there, both Jackson and Nathan were fawning over Abby. Maybe she was healthy now, but her eyes still had that glazed look, as if she were a million miles away.

"You don't have to work or think about anything," Jackson said. "Just rest and get better."

That makes sense, Melissa thought. *When Abby is better, she can do her share of the work.*

Nathan turned to Abby and asked, "About the others—"

"Leave her alone," Jackson ordered.

Nathan's jaw clenched, and he glared at the bigger teen. "We were just talking. You know, Jory and Ian are my friends. I just want to know—was anybody hurt?"

Abby began wringing her hands nervously. "I don't know. But if they're not back, we should go find them." She jumped to her feet as though she was going to search for them immediately.

She took one step and swooned. Jackson lunged to catch her. "Whoa!" he said as he guided her back to her seat. "Easy there."

She smiled gratefully at him. "Wow, I'm still really weak."

"Take it slow, all right?" Jackson cast an angry glance at Nathan, as if her fainting spell had been his fault. So far, Jackson hadn't even noticed that Melissa had joined them at the fire pit.

"That's what I said," Nathan protested. "Abby shouldn't do anything until she's totally recovered. I thought I could . . ."

Nathan might as well have been talking to the ocean, because Abby and Jackson weren't paying any attention to him. They were gazing intently at each other.

"I'm so embarrassed," Abby said. "Thanks, Jackson."

"No problem." He smiled and handed her a mango.

She took a delicate bite and asked, "How come you're in charge here?"

"They elected me," he answered humbly.

Abby nodded, looking suitably impressed.

They continued to gaze at each another as if nobody else were on the island. Having seen enough, Nathan jumped to his feet and nearly ran into Melissa. From the expression on his face, Melissa could tell that he was thinking the same thing she was.

What exactly is happening here?

THIRTEEN

Eventually, everyone got to eat lunch, not just Abby, and this was one lunch that nobody wanted to miss. The gang always ate dinner together, but they were usually scattered at the mid-day meal, with nothing formal planned. Melissa understood why everyone was present today, and it wasn't the cooking. Sometime Abby would have to tell them what happened to her, Jory, Ian, and Captain Russell, and this could be the moment.

Melissa was relieved to see that Jackson looked back to normal. He sat near Abby, but not in her lap. Eric was trying to do that. Daley was serving them, and she gave their freshest fruit and best packaged food to Abby. That girl had already eaten enough for three people today, but Melissa could forgive her that.

The way she entranced the boys was a little harder to forgive. *We've been living with these guys for a week and a half—with all our flaws and emotions exposed. Abby is mystery woman, and they're falling all over her. It's not fair.*

Abby looked at the bounty of food set before her and smiled at her helpful server. "Thanks, Daley."

"No problem," the redhead answered. "You gotta get your strength back."

Meanwhile, the others were getting no food. Eric pointed to his empty plate. "Okay, c'mon, we're dying here!"

Everyone finally got something to eat, and they chewed in relative silence. There was some talk about the new bamboo canopy, and how it was going to help protect the fire. Every few seconds, someone would look expectantly at Abby, hoping she would enlighten them. But she was too busy wolfing down her food.

Finally it was Lex who blurted, "Did you find civilization?"

That stopped all chewing and talking cold, and everyone looked at Abby. She shook her head glumly and answered, "No."

Taylor pouted in disappointment, but Nathan beat her to the next question. "So what did you find?" he asked.

Abby sighed and set down a half-eaten fig. For the first time, she looked determined to come to grips with whatever had happened to her.

Abby swallowed her food, smiled bravely, and looked at their expectant faces.

What do I tell them? My memory is just starting to come back ... in bits and pieces. The beginning is clearer to me than the end. I just can't remember very much of it. I guess the sun and the thirst cooked it out of me, or maybe I got hit harder on the head than I thought.

I didn't really do much thinking when I was walking alone in the jungle—I was just trying to get back to the plane and everyone else. I was just trying to stay alive.

Now they want me to think ... to tell them everything. But I don't know! I can't remember. All I remember are Jory's jokes and Ian's goofy smile ... oh, what happened to them?

In the beginning, we were full of confidence when we left these guys behind on the beach. Captain Russell was sure we would only be gone a couple of hours. Max.

"Man, I should have brought the machete," said Captain Russell, huffing and puffing after stumbling through the underbrush for half an hour. He was a grubby, unshaven man in a loud Hawaiian shirt, and Abby wondered if he was always this grumpy, too. Sure, crashing a plane must be hard on the pilot, but none of them had been hurt. He had made a great crash landing on the beach. So what if the radio picked up nothing but static, and they were lost?

We'll find help soon, she told herself, *then our field trip and vacation will be back on schedule. By tomorrow, we'll be sitting in a hotel room, laughing about this craziness.*

Captain Russell was the one who suggested going inland to look around, and it sounded like a good idea to Abby. Her friends, Ian and Jory, had volunteered right away, too. Ian and Jory were now trailing behind, because they had the backpacks, full of canned food, blankets, water, and other survival stuff.

The pilot took another opportunity to stop and catch his breath. It was hot and humid in the jungle, and the bugs found you quickly when you stopped moving. So Abby walked ahead on the little trail—it looked like an animal path. As long as they kept moving away from the sound of the surf, they had to be headed inland.

"Hey! Where are you going?" Captain Russell snapped.

Abby stopped and looked back at him. "Just walking. I'm not tired."

"I'm not either," Russell lied, "but we have to wait for those idiots with the backpacks to catch up. You kids remember . . . *I'm* the leader of this outfit. Don't make me sorry that I brought you, or I'll send you back to the beach. I'm serious. I don't want you kids slowing me down."

Abby suppressed a smile, because it was Captain Russell who was slowing *her* down. "All right," she answered, taking a breather. She cupped her hand around her mouth and shouted to the treetops, "Hello, anyone! Is anyone out there?"

"Oh, save your breath," the pilot muttered. "Just past this stretch of jungle, we'll find a road or something. This island is too big to be uninhabited."

"Then why weren't there tourists on the beach?" Jory asked when she caught up with them. "How come no beach chairs? No drinks with little umbrellas?" The stocky girl paused to lean against a tree trunk, trying to rest her heavy backpack.

Russell grumbled, "How do I know? Even in Hawaii, there are deserted beaches. If we just keep heading inland, we'll find something."

Ian stopped to pull an object out of the pocket of his tight jeans. Abby watched in amazement as the lanky rocker with long hair tried to dial a number on his cell phone. She laughed. "Are you getting a signal?"

"No, dude, I'm not," he answered glumly. "Not even roaming. We are so lost that we are 'Out of Service.'"

Captain Russell studied the sun peaking through the treetops. Abby followed his gaze and spotted coconuts high up in a palm tree, but she would have to have wings to get them. She decided that she should do some foraging as they hiked along. Couldn't hurt.

"Hey, maybe text messaging!" Ian said, working his phone's tiny keypad.

"Forget it, sport," the pilot muttered. "Shoe leather—that's the only thing that will get us out of here. By the position of the sun, that way is north. Any objections if we go north?"

Ian shook his head. "Nope."

"You know," Jory said, "there were cannibals in the South Pacific as recently as 1957."

"Why do I have to babysit a bunch of kids?" the pilot grumbled as he struck off in a new direction, ignoring the animal path they had been following. "I know we're going to find civilization. Maybe it won't be a resort . . . just a campground. Maybe a fishing village or a lumber yard. If we can get to high ground, we can see more of the coast."

Captain Chaos, Eric had called him, but he was focused as he drove them on an uphill climb, trying to get to this mythical high ground from which they could see the rest of the island. The resort, fishing village, whatever—it was always just over the next hill, through the next swampy meadow. Only problem was, the more they walked, the more trees, bushes, and thickets they saw.

No people. No buildings. No sign of civilization.

Finally, they trekked across a rocky plain and came to a vast canyon full of silvery waterfalls and lush growth. Unfortunately, this was the end of their trek due north, because they couldn't cross a chasm like that unless they had wings. They could only stare at it, while the shadows grew longer from the setting sun.

We're too far from the beach to make it back tonight, Abby thought, *if that's even what we want to do. We could walk along the rim of the canyon, heading east. Or go back. Those are the only options from here.*

Jory slumped to the ground and wriggled out of her heavy backpack. "You know," she said with a sigh, "it's been hard lugging all this stuff, but I'm going to enjoy dinner tonight. And the blanket."

"We can't stay here!" Captain Russell grumbled, flapping his arms in frustration. "We have to keep going." He swayed on his feet and staggered back from the edge of the chasm. The middle-aged man was dirty and sweaty and looked as if he couldn't take another step without falling on his face.

"You want to keep exploring in the dark?" Abby asked. She set down an armful of fruit she had gathered on the march and glanced at Ian and Jory. They stared back at her, breathing heavily. Nobody could take another step.

The pilot scowled, took off his shoe, and emptied the dirt out of it.

"Captain Russell," she began carefully, "we have to admit the truth. There isn't a resort or a road or anything around here. That doesn't mean we won't find it . . . or get a good view from high ground. But we won't do it *today*."

"Yeah, darn it!" Russell muttered as he sat on a rock. "Why did I ever take this stupid job? When I heard it was a bunch of kids, I should've called in sick."

"Hey, Cap, what do *we* have to do with it?" Ian asked, stretching out on the ground. "We didn't make you fly into the storm."

Russell frowned and swatted a bug on his neck. "No, but I usually fly cargo, not kids. You guys running around the cabin—you distracted me just before the storm hit. So I didn't check my heading. Geez, I hate these island hops with a bunch of whiny passengers. But what's done is done. Do you know how much paperwork I'll have to do over losing that plane?"

"I'll help you," Jory said. "Anything to get us rescued." She plucked leaves and twigs out of her unruly black hair and asked softly, "So do we keep going inland tomorrow? Or go back to the beach?"

No one answered her, and Captain Russell lowered his head and gazed at the ground with a deepening scowl. Soon Ian and Jory turned to Abby, as if she had the answer. After a moment, she shrugged and said, "It's just been one day. All of us thought this was a good idea . . . to see what's inland. It's still a good idea."

She reached down and picked up a small brownish fruit. It was too bruised to buy in a supermarket, but it looked appetizing at the moment. "Anyone for some local food? I think this is a fig. Or something closely related."

Abby looked down at the half-eaten fig in her hand, and she was back on the beach, surrounded by the other group of survivors. The ones who were still surviving. She couldn't tell them *everything*, even if she could remember all of it. But they were hungry for news ... for information about the island and their missing friends.

They were destined to be disappointed.

"Captain Russell's plan was for us to hike north," Abby said. "To the far shore. But the island is way bigger than he thought. We hacked our way through miles of really thick jungle. I've never seen so many bugs. I think most of them bit me."

Daley cringed. "Sounds horrible."

"It was worse than horrible," Abby said, fighting the memories as much as groping for them. "But you know what? Something good came out of it. I think when you go through a nightmare like that, it brings people closer together."

There were nods all around the quiet circle, and she knew they understood. "I've known Ian and Jory forever," Abby went on, "but after going through that, we've got this incredible bond. It's like ... they're part of me."

She gazed off into the distance at the crashing waves and said, "I hate being here without them."

"So what happened?" Lex asked, trying to get her back on track.

What happened? It was a question that was so easy to ask, and so hard to answer. Abby's mind held a few sketchy details, but not enough to satisfy anyone, especially herself.

"One night, we made camp on the side of a steep mountain," she answered simply, her voice trembling. "While we were sleeping, a storm hit. A big one."

"Yeah!" Nathan said. "It got us too."

How many days ago was that? It didn't matter. Her friends wanted to know everything, even if she couldn't remember more than a few disturbing details. The way they were staring at her ... Abby just wanted their attention to go away. She wanted to scream at them, *Ask about something else. I don't remember!*

Melissa looked pained by her hesitation, and Abby finally blurted the first thing she could think of. "There was a flash flood," she said. "It came so fast, crashing down the mountain. It wiped out camp and scattered our gear. I was thrown against a rock and hit my head. I think. It was so dark ... I crawled to get away from streams of water, but I didn't know which way to go."

The only sound was the crashing of the waves

as the survivors hung on her every word.

Taking a deep breath, Abby continued. "I wandered around the rest of the night in the storm. When morning finally came ... the weather cleared, but I was alone."

"Oh, man," Taylor muttered.

"I lost everything," Abby said in a hushed voice. "My gear, my food ... my friends. The only thing I could do was to look for the way back here. I was so confused. I put notes on trees, because I thought I was walking in circles. I got so weak I had to lie down. Next thing I knew, I woke up here."

Jackson frowned and asked, "So the others are still headed north?"

"I don't know." Abby stared morosely at the dense jungle. "I keep hoping to see them."

Melissa's heart went out to her friend, and she felt awful about being jealous of Abby. It was a miracle that she had found her way back, and that they had found her. The proof of that was that Ian, Jory, and Captain Russell were still missing.

Eric put a fatherly arm around Abby's shoulders and said, "As the person who found you—and technically saved your life—I feel responsible for your well-being."

"Oh, please," Daley muttered.

"Take it slow," Eric continued. "Don't do any work. I'll cover for you."

"And who will cover for you?" Nathan asked.

There was some good-natured banter, and Abby smiled again. "Thanks, everybody."

Melissa reached out and patted her friend on the shoulder. "Don't worry, you're one of us now," she said. "You're back with family."

Abby nodded, but the smile slowly faded from her lips as she gazed past Melissa at the endless stretch of trees that led to the interior.

FOURTEEN

Ian and Jory and Captain Russell ... yes, we're a family, thought Abby as more of the past trickled into her brain. Seeing Daley and Melissa and all her friends was bringing back the missing days, but it was like watching a TV show on fast-forward with the sound turned off. Blurry visions ... disjointed actions ... misty dawns that faded into black nights. It was somehow all mixed up together.

After lunch, Abby volunteered to wash clothes, which was a simple task. Brainless enough. As she laundered garments in a bucket made from the plane's nose cone, she tried to assemble the pieces of her broken memory. Like a jigsaw puzzle, one section often led to finding another, and their second day of exploration slowly took form in her mind.

Thanks to the blankets Ian and Jory had brought, they were able to sleep a little that first night in the woods. But Captain Russell woke up howling and cursing. "Something bit me!" he complained between swear words. "It hurts like hell!"

Abby lifted up his blanket, revealing a red centipede about six inches long.

"Kill it!" Russell yelled. Under the moonlight, they chased the monster bug until Jory managed to squish it with her sturdy Doc Marten boots. A few dozen of the creature's legs still twitched even after its guts oozed into the dirt.

"They're poisonous," Jory explained. "Where did it get you?"

"On my . . . on my . . ." Embarrassed, Captain Russell pointed to his rear end.

"That's good," Ian said helpfully. "Lots of meat there."

Abby suppressed a laugh, and Jory added, "It should feel like a bee sting. More or less."

"A lot *more* at the moment," growled Captain Russell. While he rubbed the sore spot, he stared at the misty clouds stretching across the vast canyon to the north. The sky was beginning to lighten around the silhouette of the towering trees behind them. Dawn would be here in a few more minutes.

"We're gonna cross that gorge," Captain Russell vowed.

"How?" Abby asked in amazement.

"I don't know . . . yet," he admitted. "But I just

know we'll find something on the other side. That's why the roads don't come over here."

If there are any roads, Abby thought, but she didn't say that. Instead, she remarked, "If your bite gets too bad, I saw some moss we can put on it."

"Moss?" Russell scoffed. "What are you, a witch doctor?"

"Well, we don't have any aspirin or ice to put on it," Abby answered. "Some moss is analgesic— it might lessen the pain."

"I'll deal," the pilot muttered. He looked at Ian, who was stretched out on his blanket as if he was going back to sleep. Russell kicked his foot. "Come on, sport, we're already up and awake. Let's get an early start. We'll go along the rim of the canyon and look for a way across. Or at least high ground."

Nobody was going to argue with a grouchy adult with a centipede bite on his behind, so they packed up their gear and headed off at first light. The terrain was rocky and treacherous, but it was easier than hacking a trail through the jungle. By the time the warm sun crept over the treetops, they had hiked a fair distance. Nobody bothered to look anymore for signs of civilization, because there weren't any.

The hours slipped by, each one marked by a new aching muscle or bug bite.

"Hey, let's play the letter game," Ian said. "I see something that starts with the letter A. Air."

"You can't see air," Jory scoffed. "I see something—an ant!" She pointed to the ground.

Ian stopped to look at the ant hill she had found. "Okay," he grumbled, "that's one for you. But I see the B—a butterfly. Over there!" He pointed to a colorful insect flitting between yellow flowers in a thicket.

"Okay, we're tied," Jory allowed.

"C," Captain Russell barked. "For children . . . spoiled ones."

"We can't include ourselves," protested Ian. "Or I could've said 'C for captain' or 'A for Abby.' "

"Or 'B for beautiful,' " Jory added, pointing to herself.

"Why don't you just say nothing at all," muttered Russell. "That would make this hike a lot more pleasant."

"D for dork," Ian whispered to Abby.

Captain Russell whirled on him. "Who you calling a dork?" the adult demanded. Ian shrank back, but there was a defiant look in the young man's eyes.

Abby quickly stepped between the two males. "Don't we have enough troubles," she asked, "without fighting among ourselves? We may be out here for days—"

"No way!" Russell snapped. "We're gonna find the road or the resort. It's just around the bend, I know it."

"Then let's get along until we do," Abby insisted. She gave Captain Russell a pointed look, and he grumbled something and walked ahead of them.

Jory sidled up to Abby and whispered, "Maybe this wasn't such a good idea."

Abby shook her head. "We can't give up after one day and a centipede sting. Do you want to sit on the beach day after day, wondering what's out here? I don't. Besides, the others are depending on us to find help."

"What if they get rescued first?" Ian asked.

"Then they'll tell the rescuers to come looking for us," Abby answered. "Who cares who gets rescued first, as long as we *all* get rescued."

"Hey!" called a gruff voice, and they saw Captain Russell waving to them from farther up the trail. "Fresh water!"

The kids ran ahead to find a muddy little stream that plunged off the cliff into a cloud of mist. Captain Russell eased his sore behind into the water, which he drank by the handful. Everyone took a greedy chug on their water bottles, because they could finally fill them. Abby considered the possibility that this water might contain nasty bacteria or parasites, but what choice did they have? For sure, it wasn't contaminated by industrial or urban waste.

She drank her fill along with the rest of them, and for the moment their mad trek into the interior didn't seem all that crazy or dangerous. *We've found water and food along the way, and we'll find help,* Abby told herself. *Tomorrow, we'll laugh about all of this.*

"That's weird," Ian said, looking toward the jungle. "What's that?"

Abby followed his gaze and couldn't see anything unusual at first. Then she spotted a black cloud floating over the stream, and it seemed to be coming closer. She thought it must be a weird fog until the others jumped to their feet and began swatting at their arms and legs. Before she could analyze the black cloud, it was on top of them.

Suddenly the air was choked with tiny insects. Gnats! They swarmed in Abby's hair, nose, mouth, and eyes. Gagging and flailing her arms, she staggered to her feet and tried to escape, but they were everywhere. Abby slipped and sprawled in the mud, but the bugs were just as thick on the ground as in the air.

Since she couldn't see and the cliff was only a few feet away, Abby decided to stay low and cover her head. From the anguished shouts of her friends, she knew they couldn't escape either.

It took forever, but slowly the bulk of the swarm moved over the cliff and mingled with the spray from the waterfall. That's what they wanted—water, not people. There were still bugs all over her, but Abby was finally able to keep them out of her eyes and nose as she crawled for dry ground. A hand gripped hers, and she saw Ian, who brushed insects out of his scraggly hair.

"This wasn't in the brochure," he sputtered, spitting out gnats. "Hey, did you see my backpack? I tripped over it."

Abby whirled around in time to see a sodden object floating down the stream. She lunged for it, but it dropped off the edge and plunged into oblivion.

Captain Russell saw it, too. "Sheesh! What's the matter with you, kid? Losing that pack!"

Ian hung his head, and Abby bit her tongue. She wanted to defend her friend, but he had lost the backpack. Russell was in a lousy mood, and there was no point making it worse. Although most of the bugs were gone by now, she could still feel residual itching on her neck and skin.

"You didn't think we even needed supplies," Jory told Captain Russell. Abby was glad to see that her friend still had her backpack, but unfortunately she still had her smart mouth, too. "You said we'd be gone a couple of hours. You've made a lot more mistakes than Ian has."

Russell wagged his finger at the girl. "I don't need any lip from you! Remember, you guys volunteered to come with me. No one figured it would be like this."

"Then let's move on," Abby blurted. "We're okay. We found water even if we lost some stuff. From now on, we'll spread out and look for food as we walk. That way . . . we'll talk less, too."

"But we're going along the cliff," Russell protested.

"No," Abby said calmly and evenly. "It's too rocky here—one of us is going to fall or twist an ankle. And there are no fruit trees around here.

We'll follow this stream, and we'll always have water. Maybe food. No matter how we look at it, we have to figure that we could be in for a long walk."

At his dark scowl, she added, "I know you're in charge, Cap. I'm just suggesting it. If there are people living in this forest, wouldn't they be near fresh water?"

Ian and Jory looked pleadingly at the captain, anxious for him to approve the new plan. Abby didn't know why the two of them should have such faith in her, but she crossed her arms and tried to be calm. It was never easy to stand up to an adult, especially a loudmouthed bully like Russell. As their pilot, he was technically in charge of them, but he had to be realistic. The original plan to take a short stroll to the resort was nonsense. That was Fantasy Island. Her suggestion was reality.

Russell snorted something and strode away from the stream. He didn't follow the edge of the cliff or the meandering flow of water, but charted a course between them. Abby let out a sigh and nodded to Ian and Jory, who spread out across the rocky plane.

Keeping one another in sight, they followed the stream until it became a marshy meadow, with thorn bushes and treacherous roots underfoot. Abby kept closest to the stream, and she fell down twice and skinned every joint on her body. She was an itchy, bloody, muddy mess, and she was glad that the nearest person was Jory, twenty feet away.

I led them this way. Can't let them see me sweat. Or cry.

They occasionally paused to pick up bruised and wormy fruit, which they ate as they walked. These stops to exchange fruit were the only times they talked, and the conversation was never about anything important. Captain Russell kept his distance and made polite comments, but Abby could see him watching her from the corner of his eye.

He's waiting for me to fail.

Despite the struggle and discomfort, the views were wonderful. Towering trees and lush ferns, brambles festooned with flowers, striped tree toads, and slithery things in the mud, which Abby learned to jump over. Tropical birds hooted and cackled at their every step, and the insects kept up a constant show of affection. Abby had welts, bites, bruises, and scratches over most of her body. The other places had rashes.

Near sunset, they found the source of the stream—a soggy bog that smelled awful and was full of reeds, bugs, and greenish scum. It almost made her sick to think they had been drinking that water. Unless they wanted to wade in a swamp up to their knees, this path had petered out.

After brushing off the ants and slugs, Ian and Rory sat down on a fallen tree trunk. They wouldn't look at Abby, but Captain Russell gave her a knowing smile.

"Hmmm," he said smugly, "that didn't pan out,

did it? But it was worth a try, I guess. Okay, Jory, you seem to know everything. You pick the next direction. Where do we go from here?"

"Uh, it's too dark to go on," the weary girl answered, who looked a lot skinnier than she had two days ago. "I suggest we get back to dry ground and make camp."

"And then?" Russell. demanded

"Then," Jory said, "we could try north again. If nothing else happens, we'll find the canyon."

Captain Russell nodded thoughtfully and cast a glance at Abby. "That's good thinking, Jory. At least one of you has some sense."

Ian cleared his throat. "Uh, dudes, we got other options, don't we? What about going back?"

"Two days we've walked," answered the pilot, "so it's two days back, even if we find the exact route we came. And you know what's back there— seven frightened kids huddling in a wrecked plane. They're depending on *us*. So I say we go on."

"But what if they're, like . . . rescued?" Ian asked. "We'd miss out on it."

"No, I think we'd see a plane flying overhead," Russell answered. "If it was a navy boat, they'd fire a gun. We haven't walked that many miles—we'd hear it. What do you think, Abby?"

She blinked at Russell, surprised to be included in his planning. In truth, she didn't know what to think anymore. It was humbling to be wrong . . . to lead them into a swamp. She wanted to make it up to her companions. Give them good advice.

"Let's go on," Abby answered softly. "But set a time limit on how far we'll go . . . without finding anyone."

"That sounds reasonable," Captain Russell agreed. "Two more days headed north. No more detours." He clapped his hands jovially. "So, gang, I see fallen wood around here. Let's build a fire!"

They found a campsite away from the swamp and got started. The teamwork of collecting wood and building a fire put them all into a better mood, and Ian and Jory were soon joking around like usual. The cheerful flames made it feel like a camping trip, plus it didn't matter so much that they only had two blankets to share among them. Just building the fire made it seem as if they were taking charge of the situation.

Abby wondered why they hadn't built a campfire last night. She supposed they were just too wiped out. They expected to find that resort over the next hill, and it was impossible to admit that they were really shipwrecked. Tonight it was easier to think of survival instead of resorts.

They ate all the food they had, but Abby's stomach still felt empty as she lay down on a bed of leaves to sleep. Total weariness and aching muscles were better sleep aids than any soft mattress, and she swiftly fell into a deep slumber.

When someone roughly shook her awake, Abby bolted upright to see burning embers popping in the darkness. "My bedroom . . . there's a fire!" she gasped with alarm.

"You're not at home, dude," a voice whispered, and she whirled around to see Ian, his long hair standing wildly on end. Half of his face glowed in the amber firelight, and the other half was dark and grim. His firm grip on her shoulder brought her back to reality.

I'm in the jungle, Abby thought with alarm. *Stranded on an island. My bedroom is far away.*

"What is it?" she asked wearily.

Ian gulped. "Captain Russell . . . he's gone."

"What do you mean . . . gone?" Abby rubbed her eyes and looked around camp. By the flickering light, she could see Jory on the other side of the fire, sleeping soundly. But Russell's bed of leaves was empty. She yawned and said, "He probably just went to the bathroom."

"For an hour?" Ian stared at her. "That's how long I've been up."

Abby stared at the black wall of trees that surrounded them on every side. She couldn't believe the pilot would really desert them in the middle of the night, but his water bottles were gone, too.

FIFTEEN

"Abby?" a male voice asked, and a firm hand shook her shoulder. "Abby, are you all right?"

"Ian!" she exclaimed, but the face staring at her was not Ian's. Too dark, hair too wild. *It's Nathan, not Ian.* Suddenly, Abby remembered where she was—on the beach, with her hands in a nose cone, washing clothes. Ian was still out there somewhere . . . in the jungle. Lost.

She jumped to her feet, anxious to do something to help her missing friends. They needed her now more than ever! The moment she took a step, she got dizzy, and Nathan had to grab her arm to steady her.

"Whoa, there!" he said with concern. "You're still not okay yet. You had better sit down and relax."

"But I've got to . . ." Abby stopped before she said anything else, because Nathan wasn't going to understand the urgency. She had almost died out there in the jungle, and she was still weak. Plus, she had no idea where her missing friends were. But they needed her help, and she was the only one who could find them.

Abby allowed Nathan to guide her back to her seat on the cooler, and she felt less dizzy as soon as she sat down. *I'll have to wait until my head clears*, she told herself.

"You're still weak," Nathan said worriedly. "I'll get you some more fruit. And water!"

He dashed off before she could tell him that her stomach was already stuffed. After living off berries and roots for a week, she had been eating constantly since they found her. But letting everyone wait on her was easier than trying to explain to them what she was going through. Her body was here, but her mind was still out there . . . with Jory, Ian, and Captain Russell.

Nathan stopped to make a brief entry in his video diary:

Wow! How scary is that? Abby's really hurting.

I feel for her, and I think I should do all I can to help her get through this thing. She may need round-the-clock attention.

Eric also picked up the camera to leave a video message for posterity:

Eric

Oh, yeah, Abby's into me. I can tell. I dig the deep chicks. They're so ... deep. And I saved her life. Did I mention I'm a hero? It's good to have a hero in the group.

If I want to close the deal with Abby, I have to find Ian and Jory, and the pilot dude. That would ice the cake. I'll have to organize a search party and teach the others how to be observant, like I am. I'll work on that this afternoon ... right after my nap.

Taylor hummed a cheery song as she carried an armload of her dirty clothes from the girls' tent to the plane, where the clothesline was strung. She was glad to see that her good buddy Abby was still happily washing clothes and hanging them on the line, and she nodded with satisfaction.

"I knew you weren't serious about that 'no work, nothing but rest' routine," Taylor said smugly. "I can tell, that's not for Abby. She wants to contribute to our little society and make herself useful."

"That's right," Abby answered with a sigh.

Taylor dumped her bundle of clothes on the sand. "Wash colors separately—we don't want bleeding—and don't wring anything dry. It makes everything all scrunchy. I hate that feeling. It's bad enough we don't have a dryer."

"Okay." Abby gazed at the jungle for a moment, and she seemed adrift in thought. A moment later, she shook it off and went back to scrubbing clothes.

Taylor clapped her hands happily and cooed, "I am so happy you're here! You're like the sister I always wanted. We are going to do everything together!"

Abby gave her a warm smile, and Taylor snapped, "Now get to work."

Taylor left her new friend at the wash bucket and waved happily to Lex as she sauntered off. *Time to take a nap.*

From his perch on the airplane, Lex looked

down at the new girl. At least Abby was new to him, although the others acted as if she was their long-lost best friend. Or girlfriend. He was amazed at the dynamics among the high-school kids. It was interesting how the addition of one could throw off the result by so much. They had a delicate balancing act before, but Abby had thrown it out of kilter.

The boys were goofy, and all of them were competing with one another for her attention. The girls had gone from being motherly to wary. Taylor was opportunistic the way she had put poor Abby to work, but she was using her old skills of the social superior. Mainly, Abby was like a fresh breeze just blowing into camp, but there was the scent of a storm in her presence.

Lex felt sorry for her—she didn't seem very happy. While all of them watched the ocean and the sky, Abby preferred to look at the jungle and the dark heart of the island.

She did Taylor's wash in a halfhearted manner and hung it at odd angles on the line, but her mind seemed in another dimension. When Abby took a short walk by herself and sat under a tree, Lex opened a canvas bag he had been saving.

"Hey!" called a familiar voice.

Lex turned to see his sister, and he waved. Daley knelt down beside him and pointed to the pile of red and white silks in his bag. "What's that?"

"It's a parachute!" Lex answered. "I thought we could spread it out, so a plane can see it from the air."

"That's a great idea," Daley said with a smile. "It might also make a sail . . . for a boat."

"I thought of that," Lex answered. "But I think that might be too dangerous. We're not at that point yet."

Daley nodded thoughtfully. "You're a smart kid. Let me help you."

The two of them began to pull the chute out of its pack, but Lex stopped when he realized that they were going to need more room. For the moment, maybe the parachute was better in its case.

"I think we have a problem, Day."

"Why?" she asked. "We just started."

"I mean Abby," the kid answered. "She's really upset."

Daley frowned and tugged at one of her pigtails. "I know. She's had a tough time."

"What do you think happened to the others?"

As soon as he saw the pained expression on his sister's face, Lex knew she had no answer. How could she? Even the one person who'd been with them didn't know.

Daley managed a brave smile and lied. "Well, they're probably safe and on their way to the north shore." Her lip trembled, and she looked down at the colorful parachute. "Let's open this thing up!"

Lex gulped down a lump in his throat. He knew they couldn't dwell on the bad stuff—they had to keep going. "Spread it all out on the beach . . . where there's more room."

"Right!" Daley answered, jumping to her feet. "You know, if we had a motorboat, we could go parasailing!"

"That would be cool!" Lex agreed with a big grin.

Abby sat on a log and let the cool sea breeze wash over her. That's one thing they all missed while they were exploring inside the island—the sound, smells, and peacefulness of the ocean. All that water was a huge barrier, but it made her feel connected to the rest of the world. Wandering around the vast interior of the island only made her feel small and helpless.

She recalled that second night in the jungle, when Captain Russell deserted them and disappeared into the darkness. Or so they thought.

The amber light of the campfire only penetrated a few feet into the trees, where it was swallowed in blackness. A handful of bats flitted through the branches and swooped over the flames, making Abby duck.

She looked worriedly at Ian and whispered, "Where did he go?"

The rocker shrugged. "I don't know. When I woke up, he was gone, and I couldn't sleep. I decided to wait an hour before I got worried enough to wake you up. Do you want to go look for him?"

"Look for him?" Abby pointed into the utter darkness all around them. "We don't even have a flashlight."

She paced nervously around the campfire, almost tripping over Jory's sleeping figure. Abby threw another log onto the fire, shooting embers into the sky, but the light and warmth weren't much comfort. Finally, she just cupped her hand to her mouth and shouted, "Captain Russell! Where are you?"

"Huh?" Jory muttered, blinking awake. The girl sat up and stared sleepily at Abby. "Is this the Girl Scout troop?" she asked.

"No," Abby answered. "This is the shipwrecked troop."

"Oh, yeah," Jory mumbled, brushing her hair out of her eyes. "I almost forgot there . . . for a moment. Where's the captain?"

"That's what we're trying to figure out." Abby cupped her hand around her mouth and yelled again. "Captain Russell!"

"Keep your pants on!" a distant voice called. "I'll be there in a second."

Abby let out a sigh of relief as she peered into the darkness. Finally, the disheveled figure of the pilot shuffled into the firelight, limping slightly. In his hand were two beautiful pale-yellow orchids, and the sight of them stunned Abby into silence.

"Where were you?" Ian blurted. "You had us worried."

"Two things," the pilot answered. "I wanted to get a look at the stars away from the light, and I had to pick these." Proudly, he held up the beautiful flowers, which looked so waxy and perfect that they might have been fake. "Night-blooming orchids. Dendrobiums, I think. I saw them back in the marsh, and I was determined to see if they had bloomed. They had."

Russell laughed at their stunned expressions. "Surprised that a guy like me could like flowers?"

"You should have told someone," Abby said crossly. "We were worried about you."

"Aw, come on," he answered. "You were worried about yourselves. Don't sweat it. I took a bearing on the stars, and now I have a good idea which way is due north." Russell limped back to his makeshift bed and grimaced as he sat down.

"What's the matter with your leg?" asked Jory.

He waved in dismissal. "Nothing. I just tripped over a root, that's all. You know, you girls could wear these flowers in your hair. In the South

Pacific, a flower worn over the right ear means you're available."

Jory snorted. "I'm available for any sailor who wants to rescue me."

"I hear ya." Russell chuckled and stretched out on his bed of leaves. With the orchids resting on his chest, he looked like a dead man, and Abby felt a chill.

Why does a cheerful Russell bother me more than a grumpy one?

Abby slept fitfully the rest of the night, and her bumps and bruises felt worse in the morning. They got an early start as usual, headed north, and they were even more diligent looking for food than the day before. That was partly because Captain Russell was still limping, and she worried that he had hurt his leg more than he let on.

The pilot wore his colorful orchids over both ears. In his loud Hawaiian shirt, he looked like he was going native fast. *None of us look very good in our torn and dirty clothes*, thought Abby. *Maybe we all need some orchids.*

Conversation dwindled to a few words when they exchanged food or made bathroom stops. They had broadened their diet to include roots and berries, but none of it was very filling when they had to make their way uphill through miles of thick brush. Abby didn't complain, but it was beginning to seem as if they could walk for a week before finding anything but thorns and snakes. She tried to remember the few landmarks they passed, in case they had to retrace their steps, but one palm tree looked a lot like another.

Ian and Jory were fantastic, because they were both upbeat people. They never complained, and they always tried to be considerate and helpful. Captain Russell didn't complain much, either, but why should he? They were taking the route he wanted.

During one stop, Abby noticed that Ian had a small pad of paper and was making notes. "Have you got much paper?" she asked him.

"Just this pad," he answered. "Good thing it was in my pocket when I lost my backpack."

"You might want to save some sheets," Abby suggested.

"Why?"

She shrugged. "I don't know. What if we have to write a note to someone? Or make a map?"

"I hadn't thought of that." With a smile, Ian handed her the pad and pencil. "You keep it."

"Me, but—"

"Yeah, you," he insisted with a smile. "You've got more sense than I do. I was just writing down song lyrics."

Abby took the paper and pencil and tucked them into her back pocket. "Thanks. I won't use it unless I have to. I wish I had brought my journal."

"I know you like to write," Ian said with a grin. "When this is all over, you can write a best seller."

Abby smiled. "I hope this adventure gets boring real soon. Like ... sitting-around-a-hotel-room boring."

"I hear ya."

Toward the end of a very long day, she noticed that Russell was limping worse than before. Plus, he was in a sour mood because they hadn't found the canyon again, just more and more tropical forest. Unending tropical forest. Abby doubted whether they had walked more than half a dozen miles all day, because they made such poor time in the rough terrain.

Although they had agreed to explore for four days, it was beginning to seem pointless after three. There was not even the slightest sign of civilization. Not a path, not an abandoned hut—nothing. Abby began to feel more and more like some ancient explorer set loose in an uninhabited wilderness, only they didn't have enough supplies for a trek like this.

"I can't understand it," Russell grumbled. "We're heading north for sure, but where's that stupid canyon?"

"The canyon doesn't necessarily go in a straight line," Abby answered. "And neither do we."

"Tomorrow we'll find it," vowed Russell, his jaw set in determination. Then he winced as he slumped to the ground and rubbed his leg. "Anyway, we're done for today."

Without warning, Jory doubled over and

vomited violently, and Abby jumped back and stared in alarm.

"Oh, man!" Ian exclaimed, hovering over his friend. "Are you okay?"

"Do I look okay?" Jory croaked. "I didn't say anything before, but ... actually I feel better now. Sure wish I had a toothbrush and toothpaste, though."

Abby looked worriedly at her friend and bent down to help her to her feet. While she did, she touched her friend's forehead—it was clammy and hot. "Let's find another place to camp."

"This is okay here," said Captain Russell, stretching out on the ground. "I'm not moving. Just kick some leaves over the barf."

"Probably something I ate," murmured Jory as Abby conducted her to a log several feet away from the scene of the sickness. Now Abby's stomach felt a little queasy, too, and she wondered about all the raw roots and wormy fruit they had eaten, not to mention the untreated water. It might only be a matter of time before they were all in this condition.

As darkness draped over the trees, a gloom descended upon the weary foursome huddled in the jungle. There was nothing left to eat and very little water left to drink. Captain Russell looked like he was asleep, and Abby kept her arm around Jory's shoulders. The poor girl was shivering, even though she felt warm.

No one spoke for a long time until Ian cleared his throat. "Uh, dudes," he began, "do you think maybe we should punt?"

"Punt?" Russell asked, his eyes still shut. "Do you mean . . . quit?"

"I mean, we could wander around for a week and not see anything but this." Ian motioned at the darkening forest while birds cackled in the trees.

"He's got a point," Abby said softly.

"No, he doesn't," countered Russell. "What do you suppose those kids back on the beach are eating? Roast beef and cherry pie? Do you really want to sit on this island and rot, or do you want to do something to get us rescued? I already know the answer to that, or else you wouldn't be here."

"I'm okay," Jory said weakly. "He's right, the others are probably struggling, too. Really . . . I feel a lot better after hurling."

"One more day," Abby reminded them all. "That's all we agreed to look."

"Get some sleep," Captain Russell said, rolling over. "We're going to cover a lot of ground tomorrow."

Abby sighed and looked at her feverish friend. Jory frowned at her and whispered, "We'll be okay, right?"

"Yeah," answered Abby, mustering a smile. "Yeah, I'm sure we'll be okay." She glanced at the trees, knowing the bats would be swooping soon.

SIXTEEN

Melissa hung out by the fire pit near the beach, doing her water chores—filtering, boiling, and pouring. In between those tasks, she made more coconut-shell candles, although it didn't seem like anyone was too impressed by them. Whenever she tried to demonstrate her candles, their eyes glazed over.

Wait until the batteries finally give out, Melissa thought. *Then they'll appreciate my candles.*

She heard male voices, and she turned to see Eric headed toward the fire pit with a tray of fruit in his hands. Nathan dogged after him.

"Hey, what's that for?" Nathan demanded, sounding suspicious.

Eric moved faster than Melissa had ever seen him move, as he grabbed a bottle of water from her crate and headed toward the airplane. "Abby," he replied nobly. "She needs some tender loving Eric-care."

Nathan cut him off and said, "Uh, yeah, I'll bring it to her."

"I picked it, I'll take it to her," answered Eric stubbornly. He held the tray away from Nathan and tried to get around him.

"Eric, she's upset," Nathan pleaded, "and she trusts me. We've already started to bond."

Eric squinted doubtfully at him. "Bond? I saved her life! *That's* a bond!"

"Gimme a break," Nathan said. "You saw a note on a tree." He made a lunge for the tray of food and water, but Eric eluded him.

"Whatever, I'm responsible," Eric insisted.

"No, you're not. I'm going to—"

Before Nathan could finish with his threat, Jackson appeared from nowhere and stepped between them. "What's the problem?" he asked.

Melissa could tell him in one word—Abby— but Jackson wouldn't want to hear it.

"There's no problem," answered Nathan. "We just want to help Abby."

Jackson nodded as though this was a good idea, and he deftly grabbed the tray away from Eric. "I can do that." He left the other two boys gaping as he strode toward the plane, where Abby was listlessly washing clothes.

"How did that happen?" Eric asked in shock.

Melissa only wanted to know what was going to happen next. While Eric and Nathan argued over whose fault it was that Jackson would get the glory, Melissa slipped out the back way and ran from the fire pit to the trees. Hidden and at a distance, she watched Jackson approach the wrecked plane with his stolen offering.

Melissa had plenty of cover to steal down from the trees and get close enough to listen to their conversation. She felt a bit like Eric, snooping on them, but this was an emergency.

Abby looked spaced out until Jackson sat beside her. Then she went back to scrubbing clothes in the old nose cone. "Aren't you supposed to be taking it easy?" asked Jackson with concern.

"I am," she answered, holding up a dripping shirt. "Taylor and I are going to be sharing her clothes."

He gently took her hand and removed it from the washtub. "It's okay, Cinderella. Taylor can wash her own clothes. I brought you some food and water."

Abby smiled gratefully at him and leaned back in the sand. She tried looking at the ocean, but her attention never drifted very far from the tree line. Jackson noticed it, too.

"Your head's back in the jungle with them, isn't it?" he asked.

She nodded gravely. "I feel so guilty. I'm sitting here on a beautiful beach, all safe, and they're . . ." She couldn't finish her thought.

Jackson smiled reassuringly. "They're probably just as worried about you."

"I feel like I abandoned them." Abby's lower lip trembled, and she looked down at the sand.

Watching from her hiding place, Melissa felt guilty for eavesdropping. Abby was dealing with an awful lot right now, and all the attention from the boys was probably more annoying than exciting. Jackson was just trying to be sympathetic, she hoped.

This wasn't Abby, anyway. Abby was vivacious, fun, and a little goofy. Abby believed in astrology and wanted to tell your fortune. This person who had crawled back to them through the jungle seemed troubled and needy. Was that the reason everybody responded to her like they did? Like she was a sick puppy who needed care.

"I don't pretend to have answers about anything," Jackson finally told her. "But there's one thing I've learned since we got dumped here."

"What's that?" Abby graced him with a smile.

"You can't control the unknown," he answered. "If you stress over what might happen, it'll tear you apart. It's about right here, right now."

Tenderly, he stroked her back. "You're safe with us. That's all that matters."

Abby and Jackson gazed warmly into each other's eyes, while Melissa caught her breath. This talk didn't seem so therapeutic anymore, and she had seen way more than she wanted to see. Was this

the famous Jackson who was so weighed down
by the rigors of command that he couldn't think
about romance? Yep, same one. The one making
smoochy eyes at Abby, who was too weak to stand
up.

Melissa didn't know whether to cry, laugh, or
hit him in the head with a coconut. Gulping down
a lump in her throat, she ran back to the fire pit.

From the corner of her eye, Abby saw Melissa
running down the beach . . . away from her and
Jackson. There wasn't much reason for anyone to
run on this island. For the first time, Abby realized
that things weren't as simple in this camp as they
appeared to be.

*Three girls, three boys, not counting Daley's
little brother. That might mean trouble—boy-girl
trouble. What have I stepped into?*

"So we learned to fish," Jackson was saying.
"Can you believe it, Taylor was the only one who
knew anything about fishing."

"Yeah," Abby answered distractedly. "Um, I'd
really like to talk, but I've got to get this washing
done. Like you say, Taylor kinda runs this island."

"No, she doesn't," Jackson protested. He
reached into the bucket for a sopping pair of
shorts. "Let me help you."

"No," Abby said firmly. "You've done enough.

Everybody has done enough. It's time for me to do my share."

"But I want to tell you all the stuff we've been doing to get rescued."

Please go away, she wanted to say. *The past is coming back to me now . . . in a rush. I've got to have space and time to put it all together.*

"Let me eat the food you brought me," she told Jackson. "We'll talk more later."

Looking disappointed, Jackson nodded and rose to his feet. "If you need anything, anything at all . . ."

She granted him a smile. "I know. Call you."

"Yeah." He pointed down the beach. "I've got some chores to do, but I won't be far away."

"We'll be okay," Abby assured him with a smile.

Isn't that the same thing I told Jory? We'll be okay. But we weren't okay.

Jackson's brow furrowed. "You know, if we collect enough food, some of us can go look for Jory, Ian, and the pilot."

That comment was like a kick in the stomach, and Abby looked worriedly at the trees, their leaves waving gently in the breeze. From here, the island looked so benign and pretty, when it was really a treacherous wilderness.

When she said nothing, Jackson took that as his cue to leave. "Okay, see you in a bit."

"Yeah, thanks." Abby forced a smile.

As Jackson walked off into the bright sunlight, she remembered the dark clouds that swirled over their heads on that fateful day. She didn't even know how many days ago it was, but she remembered the ominous sky that formed over the small band of explorers.

"Surfer clouds," Ian called them. He studied the gray patches of sky visible between the tall treetops. "Back home, clouds like that mean good surf. But for us, it probably means rain."

"Yeah." Abby nodded and looked back at Captain Russell and Jory, who were bringing up the rear. Russell still hadn't shown her his injured leg, but his limp was getting worse. Jory had been sick twice that day and couldn't keep any food down. Of course, the food they had was hardly worth keeping down. They were bravely trudging along, helping one another.

I should stop this craziness, thought Abby. But stopping here in the middle of the jungle wouldn't do them any good. They would still have to hike three or four days just to get back to the beach, and half their party didn't look as if they could walk another mile. *Oh, please, let us find help. Let us get rescued.*

They trudged onward, and nothing changed, except for the terrain and plant life. As they started uphill again, the trees grew smaller and the ground became rockier. Captain Russell got a burst of energy and caught up with the leaders. "We're coming to the canyon!" he said excitedly. "I can feel it."

"What are we going to do when we get there?" Abby asked.

"Cross it," he said stubbornly. "There's nothing on this side of the island, that's for sure. Just follow me."

"Okay," she agreed.

With the males in the lead again, Abby dropped back to keep Jory company. Her usually jolly friend looked pale and miserable, and she held her stomach as she walked. Abby took her backpack from her.

"You guys should just leave me here," said Jory with a sigh. "Pick me up on the way back."

"No way," snapped Abby. "We're not splitting up any more than we already are. And we sure aren't going to leave anyone alone out here. We *all* go forward ... or none of us."

Jory sighed. "I'd say we could send Ian and the captain ahead, but he's worse off than I am. I think that sore on his leg is infected."

"Really?" Abby asked with concern. "Why does he have to be so macho?"

"Oh, he feels pretty lousy about the plane crash. Wants to redeem himself."

"Well, he can't do that by killing himself."

Jory snorted a laugh. "Well, what are the rest of us doing?"

Abby nodded glumly, because she couldn't argue with that. They were wandering blindly, looking for the old needle in the haystack. And what a haystack this wild island was.

Toward the end of the day, a slight drizzle began to fall on the weary explorers, and the wind picked up fiercely. The cool weather was a refreshing change from the humid jungle, but Abby was worried that they had no shelter on this plain. At least in the forest, the massive trees offered some protection from the rain.

"I see it!" Russell shouted jubilantly. "The canyon!"

If he found a Holiday Inn, that would be exciting, Abby thought.

She took Jory's arm and helped her pick up the pace. A minute later, they stood beside Ian and Russell, gazing into the depths of a wide gorge. From here, the canyon didn't look as deep or as steep as when they first discovered it. The chasm was like a dividing line across the island, thought Abby, so maybe it was possible that a separate world lay on the other side.

There wasn't even a cliff—just a slope that descended into the gorge. It didn't look impossible to cross, and the first half of the trek would be all downhill. Three days ago, they could have crossed it easily. Now she wasn't so sure.

"Hey, look, here's an animal path," said Russell as he limped downward.

"Are you sure you're up to this?" Abby asked.

Russell gaped at her. "Are you kidding? On the other side of that canyon is salvation. Can't you feel it?"

Stepping carefully over the rocky terrain, they started down the narrow animal path. They picked their way around the scraggly bushes and jagged outcroppings, slipping occasionally. With his bad leg, Russell had problems keeping up, but he was more determined than anyone else. Abby knew they couldn't make it all the way across in the fading light of this day, and she wondered where they would camp.

Still, it was a relief going downhill, and the cool drizzle was refreshing. Abby kept glancing upward at the swirling gray clouds, made even blacker by the coming of night. If it began to rain hard, this rugged slope could turn into slick mud. Unfortunately, they were halfway between the top and the bottom. When thunder rolled across the vast chasm and rain splattered her face, Abby knew they were in trouble.

"Stop!" she called. "We've gotta make camp. We've gotta get ready for this storm."

"Hey, a little rain never hurt anyone," countered Russell. "It's not even dark yet. We can make it to the bottom before nightfall."

"Where we'll get caught in a flash flood," said Jory. "I think Abby's right."

Russell whirled to face the girls, anger blazing

in his eyes. "Yeah, but *I'm* in charge, not Abby! She's been trying to take over this operation ever since we left the beach, but *I'm* the adult. I'm responsible for you."

Abby's lips thinned, and Ian and Jory looked sheepishly at their feet. Finally, Abby took a deep breath and said, "We all volunteered to come with you, that makes us all responsible. If you wanted to do this alone, you should've said so. Now you need us, and we need you. We're all in this together."

"Dude, I don't like the look of those clouds," said Ian. "I think it would be a good idea to go back to the top."

"Go back?" Russell snorted in derision. "If you want to give up, be my guest. Me, I'm going to find—"

His words were drowned out by an ear-shattering crack of thunder that made all of them jump. Captain Russell scowled at the gathering clouds and began limping down the trail in a hurry. By now, the drizzle had turned the slope into a muddy mess, and he took only a few steps before his feet slipped out from under him.

Abby, Ian, and Jory watched in horror as Captain Russell tumbled down the steep chasm.

SEVENTEEN

Melissa tried not to get angry over the way Abby and Jackson were "bonding." All the boys were falling over themselves to help the girl recover from her grim experience, and Jackson was no better or worse than the others. It's just that Abby seemed more attracted to him than she did to Eric or Nathan, and Melissa could understand that. Maybe the novelty of a damsel in distress would wear off in a day or two.

If it doesn't, I'll just have to move on, she decided, although it would be horrible to see Abby and Jackson making goo-goo eyes at each other every day. All day long.

Melissa busied herself making more coconut-shell candles. She made a few improvements in her latest design, including a bracket, cut from scrap metal, to hold the wick in place. Proudly, Melissa lit one of her new candles and gazed at the primitive flame. Anything that brought light to this mysterious island was welcome.

We all worry we won't be rescued, but what will we be like when we do get rescued? High school is going to seem awfully tame after this. Are promises made here any good back there? That's a different planet than this one.

A thud sounded inside the airplane, which made her jump. Catching her breath, Melissa remembered that Nathan was supposed to be cleaning up inside the cabin. The boys had made a mess in there last night, doing something. She waited patiently for him to finish, because she wanted to show her candle to someone.

When Nathan came out, she proudly held up her newest creation. "Hey! Check out my—"

"Look what I found!" crowed Nathan, holding out a small journal. "Abby's notebook. It was still in her seat pocket. This'll cheer her up."

"My candle . . ." Melissa said, but Nathan was already hurrying off to find Abby.

Melissa grumbled and set down her candle. She caught sight of Taylor strolling past the plane, and she didn't look very busy.

"Taylor!" called Melissa. "Could you help me get more oil for my candles?"

Taylor smiled blithely and waved her off. "Sorry, talk to Abby."

"Abby," muttered Melissa, her eyes narrowing

in anger. "Abby, Abby, Abby . . . it's all about Abby."

Gripping her lighted candle in her hand, Melissa stood up and stalked across the beach. All the boys seemed to be wandering around camp, looking for Abby, so Melissa joined the search. She didn't know what she was going to say to her friend, but she was tired of sitting around and doing nothing.

When she spotted Jackson at the fire pit, she figured that Abby couldn't be far away. Sure enough, the girl came strolling out of the jungle, looking relaxed and happy. Melissa stood behind a tree and watched as her friend made straight for their leader.

Abby was all smiles when she called, "Jackson!" He turned around and grinned at Abby, obviously glad to see her.

"I've been doing a lot of thinking about what you said," she continued, "and I think you're right."

"Yeah? Right about what?" Jackson asked.

Abby walked up to him and gazed longingly into his eyes, which was too much for Melissa. Whatever Jackson was right about, it looked wrong to her! *Didn't he tell me straight-up that he couldn't handle a romance until we got home? Abby suddenly showing up doesn't make this Los Angeles!*

Melissa charged up to the pair and planted herself between them. "Excuse me," she snapped. "Am I missing something here?"

Jackson tried to play innocent. "What do you mean?"

Melissa felt like gesturing wildly, so she set her lighted candle on the ground. "Are you two, like . . . flirting?" she asked accusingly.

"What?" Jackson asked. "No."

"No." Abby shook her head, but she looked hurt at Melissa's outburst of jealousy.

Suddenly Eric ran up to the fire pit and said, "Hey, if there's any flirting going on, I should be involved."

Jackson smiled. "You're not even my type."

"Abby!" called another male voice. Nathan came running up, and all of Abby's suitors had her surrounded, which didn't do anything to mollify Melissa.

Nathan shoved the diary under Abby's nose. "Look, I found your notebook. Isn't that great?"

"Uh, thanks," she muttered, looking over-whelmed at all the attention.

Melissa didn't care about the other silly boys, but now that she had made a fool of herself, she might as well let Jackson have it. She stood in front of him and put her hands squarely on her hips.

"What happened to not wanting to make things weird by having relationships here?" demanded Melissa.

Jackson laughed nervously and said, "Well, I . . . I . . ."

Before he could think of a lame response, Taylor stormed up to Abby and shook a handful of damp clothes in her face. "Abby!" she cried. "You left my clothes on the beach! What kind of sister are you?"

The girl gulped and backed away from the mob of people. "I . . . I'm sorry. I didn't think—"

Eric jumped in front of Abby. "Hey, remember me? The guy who saved your life? I sorta thought we could have a nice quiet dinner."

"She's wearing *my* clothes," protested Taylor. "She owes *me* more than you."

"Leave her alone," ordered Jackson, which goaded Melissa to jump in again.

"What about you and Abby?" she demanded. "Is romance okay on this island or not?"

"Let Abby choose whoever she wants," Nathan said.

The scene around the fire pit descended into bedlam, with everyone talking at once and Abby shrinking back from all the noise. Nobody noticed when Jackson accidentally kicked Melissa's candle, and the fiery oil splattered onto the corner pole of the new canopy. Glittering flames climbed the dry bamboo like lava flowing uphill, and the fire soon lapped at the thatched roof. Still, the argument went on, raging louder than the flames.

From the jungle, Daley blinked her eyes in amazement. The new canopy over the fire pit was on fire, and half a dozen people were standing around, arguing about something else! Not a single one of them seemed to notice that the flames were spreading wildly, only a few feet away from them. In seconds, fiery embers would collapse on their heads.

Lex tugged on her shirt. "Whoa!" he said. "We gotta—"

"I know!" Waving frantically and yelling at the top of her lungs, Daley charged toward the group. "Hey! Look out! *Fire!*"

"The canopy's on fire!" Lex shouted. "Hey! Look out!"

Finally, the heated conversation stopped, and the teenagers stared in Daley's direction. That's when they saw the fire consuming the bamboo poles and palm thatching of their newest structure. They barely had time to run out from under the canopy before fiery cinders began to rain down. One of the burning poles fell over, and the roof collapsed into the fire pit, feeding more fuel to the inferno. Flames licked the trunk of a nearby palm tree.

"Quick!" Nathan shouted. "If it spreads to the jungle, we're done!"

"Water!" Jackson yelled.

Unfortunately, most of their bottled water was under the burning canopy. Everyone grabbed whatever containers they could find and rushed to the ocean to fill them. There was frantic activity as the survivors did their best to battle the spreading flames.

Daley waded through the heat and smoke to stamp out some burning embers in the forest. When the heat grew too intense and she could smell her boots melting, she staggered out of the flames. Others tried to douse the trees with water to prevent the fire from spreading, but it was like chasing liquid lightning. They formed a fire line, passing buckets from the ocean to the fire, but it seemed as if they were losing.

More of them had to brave the smoke to stamp out the fire with their feet. People screamed and called for help to catch new flare-ups. Daley caught a lungful of smoke and collapsed to her knees in a coughing fit. The entire camp was in jeopardy, along with every pitiful possession they owned.

"More water!" shouted Jackson. "Everyone!"

Seven of them fell into a line between the surf and the fire, and the bucket brigade finally got organized. They left it to Jackson to brave the blaze and toss the water where it was needed most, and slowly the flames turned into smoldering gusts of smoke.

Five minutes later, Daley lay slumped in the sand, exhausted and panting. Dark clouds of smoke hung over the camp, and the survivors stared at the remains of their fire pit. They were in shock, numb. Quick action had saved most of the nearby foliage, but there was nothing left of the canopy except for some charred sticks and bits of ash wafting on the breeze. The air smelled the way Daley felt—foul and devastated.

She crossed her arms and stared at her chagrined friends. "Okay, who was the idiot who lit a fire outside the pit?"

"It was a candle," Melissa said glumly. "If Jackson wasn't all gaga over Abby, he wouldn't have kicked it over and—"

"I'm not gaga over Abby," snapped Jackson. But the way he scowled, Daley knew that he felt partly responsible.

Taylor scoffed. "The roof was a stupid idea, anyway. Of course it burned."

"It wasn't stupid," Nathan countered. "It was to protect the fire."

"And what was supposed to protect the roof?" Eric asked.

Soon they were arguing again over whose fault it was. Daley rubbed her aching head, feeling incredibly saddened by the loss. It wasn't just a few scorched poles and some melted water bottles—it was the idea that they could fail so badly. A week's worth of sacrifice, hard work, and clear thinking could be cut down in one moment of stupidity.

It felt wrong to blame anyone for the fire, especially Abby. But this wouldn't have happened if there were still just the seven of them. Adding one more person had skewed their fragile community in a weird direction. That thought was more troubling to Daley than all the arguing and finger-pointing. They were so close to being a team . . . yet so close to breaking apart.

Daley whistled loudly, halting the squabble. "Will everyone just shut up for a moment? To err is human, but this is ridiculous."

The others looked sheepishly at her, and Daley

did a quick head count. *Lex, Jackson, Eric, Nathan, Taylor, Melissa, and me. We're all present and accounted for, except for our newest member.*

"Where's Abby?" she asked.

They looked puzzledly at one another, but nobody had an answer. "I'll go look for her," offered Nathan.

"No," snapped Daley. "There's been enough worrying about Abby. And you can't blame her for wanting to get away from us for a while. Let's do what we can to clean up this mess."

"We'll need to find more wood right away," Melissa said. "I'll get on it."

"I'll help you," Jackson offered.

Taylor looked horrified. "You don't think Abby ran off . . . wearing my clothes?"

"I see her," Lex said, peering into the distance. "She's just sitting by the plane."

"Okay, let's give her some space," Daley ordered, and nobody argued with her.

Seated on a box in the shadow of the plane, Abby put her head in her hands and listened to the soft whisper of the waves a few feet away. *Maybe I'm just a jinx*, she thought. *Wherever I go, disaster follows me.*

A second voice in her head protested: *No, girl, it's not your fault, none of it. You held that group together out there in the jungle. That night, you did everything possible to save them. It's not your fault that you got separated or that you got hit on the head. Or that you survived. It's not your fault that you got back, and they didn't. The instinct for survival is too strong.*

Abby wiped a tear from her cheek as she relived her final hours with Jory, Ian and Captain Russell.

As it rained on the side of the canyon, and the thunder roared overhead, she and Ian scrambled down the muddy slope toward Russell's limp body. The pilot had rolled at least fifty feet down the embankment, and he was pinned between a boulder and a thorn bush. They had left Jory higher up, protecting their remaining supplies and blankets— it sure looked like they would need them.

With every drop of rain, the ground got more slippery, and Abby felt as if she were on skis. Ian took a tumble, and she had to grab his hand to keep him from a dangerous fall. Now they were both on the ground, in danger of winding up like Captain Russell. Ian slid on his belly, gripping roots and bushes for support, while Abby slid on her rear end. Within seconds, her hands were raw and bloody from clawing her way down, but she never thought about stopping.

Every inch they got closer to the pilot, the more she dreaded what they would find. The captain wasn't moving, and the rain mingled with his blood to turn his Hawaiian shirt pink. "Captain Russell!" she shouted, hoping against all logic that he would respond.

He didn't, but his shoulder twitched.

"Dude's alive!" Ian shouted joyfully. He squeezed her hand, and she gripped back.

A peal of thunder crashed overhead, and Abby looked up to see that the clouds were sinking lower into the gorge. They would soon be shrouded in fog. Lightning strobed behind the gray curtain of mist, and the rain began to pound them harder. It seemed as if the whole island wanted to punish them for trying to solve its mysteries.

A few more feet! Almost there.

Gripping each other as fiercely as they hung onto roots and rocks, Abby and Ian finally reached the injured pilot. It was so steep here that Abby had to brace her feet against the boulder to keep from falling farther, and Ian wrapped his legs around the shrub. Once they had secured their positions, they turned their attention to Russell.

Abby gripped his damp wrist and felt for a pulse, while Ian grabbed his shoulder. "Don't move him," warned Abby, "until we see how bad he is."

"If he's hurt bad, what will we do?" asked Ian.

She shook her head. Not moving him was good advice back in that other world, the one they had left behind. No helicopter was coming to airlift him out. Abby tried to ignore the rain and the cold and aches in her own body to check if a pulse of life still flowed through the pilot's body.

Feeling a faint throb, she shouted, "Yes!"

Russell groaned and turned his head slightly to look at her. Blood streamed from a cut on his forehead, and his nose looked swollen and broken. "It'll take more than that to kill me," he said weakly.

"I bet," answered Abby with a grin. She looked around and realized that the boulder they were perched on was about as much shelter as they were going to get on this mountain, in this storm. Like it or not, this lousy muddy slope was going to be their camp for the night.

"Anything broken?" asked Ian.

"Probably," grumbled Russell. "My ribs are killing me . . . and my head. My leg was already messed up."

"You try to stay still," Abby said. "We're going to camp here, and we'll rig up something to keep you dry."

The pilot sniffed back a tear and looked pleadingly at her. "I'm sorry. I screwed up . . . again."

She brushed strands of gray hair off Russell's bloody forehead. "We all succeed together, or we all screw up together. We're a team, right?"

"Yeah," he croaked. He squeezed her hand.

Abby took a deep breath and turned to Ian. "You stay with him. I'm going to bring Jory down here."

"You sure? I can do it."

She patted him on the shoulder. "I got it, okay?"

"Okay, boss." Ian gave her a grateful smile.

Rain pounding her face, Abby braced herself for the climb up the slippery embankment. She dug her toes into the slop, grabbed a handhold on a rock, and started toward Jory. The rain and fog were so dense now that she couldn't even see her friend fifty feet away, so she shouted as she climbed.

"Jory! You there?"

"Yeah, yeah! Should I come down?"

"No, wait for me! I'll guide you!" Abby didn't stop to think about what she was doing—she just kept clawing her way through the rain, mud, and bushes until she reached Jory, who stood on the narrow path, shivering.

Jory helped her to her feet and hugged her. "Oh, gosh, am I glad to see you! How's Captain Russell?"

"Alive. Hurt. Wet," answered Abby. "We're going to wait out the storm . . . down there. Here, give me your backpack."

"I can carry it," protested Jory.

"No, you concentrate on getting down. I know the way better than you." Abby glanced at the violent sky while Jory took off her backpack, and she wondered if the storm would ever let up. Hard rain had turned the craggy slope into one vast mudfall, and the footing was getting worse.

Jory started to walk down, and Abby grabbed her arm. "Get on your stomach. Slide down, and hang on to roots, rocks, whatever you can find. I'll be right behind you."

The girl gulped and nodded. A moment later,

the two of them were clawing and sliding through the muck, picking up a dozen new scratches and bruises. Abby struggled with the backpack, but she knew they needed every item in there, especially the blanket. When Jory slipped, Abby grabbed her by the hand and steadied her. When Abby went into free fall, Jory grabbed her by the ankle. Shivering with panic, they held each other until they felt confident enough to move again.

A bolt of lightning helped them spot the guys at the boulder, and they changed course in order to reach them. Abby was glad to see that Ian had made the captain comfortable—or as comfortable as possible. With the wind howling and the rain slashing, Abby tried to erect a makeshift canopy from the blanket, but it kept blowing away.

"Never mind!" shouted Ian. "We're already soaking."

But Abby was determined, and she found enough rocks to anchor the blanket on top of the boulder and enough sticks to stake the corners into the ground. Panting from exhaustion, she slumped back into the mud and huddled with her comrades, their backs against the boulder.

Captain Russell squeezed her shoulder and rasped, "Good job, kid."

Numbly, Abby nodded. They weren't exactly dry or safe, but most of the rain rolled off the blanket instead of hitting them directly. As night fell and total darkness enveloped them, the only illumination was an occasional flash of lightning. In this surreal setting, Abby dozed fitfully while the hard rain faded back into a steady drizzle.

I thought we were in the clear, mused Abby. *I thought I had saved us. Yeah, right.*

She poked her big toe into the sand on the beach and looked around. Jackson, Taylor, and the others were finally giving her some space and leaving her alone. She could see them gathered around the fire pit, trying to rebuild the canopy.

Until now, those final minutes in the canyon had been a blank. They were still mostly blank, but Abby had lived in Southern California long enough to know about mudslides. So she could piece together what had happened next, even if she never saw it coming.

EIGHTEEN

Only one thing stood out in Abby's memory—the awful noise. An unearthly growl that sounded like some primordial beast rising from the depths of the earth shook her awake. The ground trembled under her, even the rocks and trees, and she opened her eyes to see a black wave come crashing down the slope into their fragile sanctuary.

Screams! Somebody grabbed her arm, but his or her fingers were ripped away. A ton of mud smashed her in the face and slammed her head against the boulder. Before she passed out, Abby instinctively covered her face with her hands, and that was probably the only thing that saved her life. That and the boulder that forced the landslide to ooze around it.

In a daze, she clawed her way through the mud and debris until she tasted fresh damp air. It was all survival instincts after that—an agonizing crawl through the darkness and the rain. Abby couldn't remember even thinking about her companions until she reached the rim of the mountain and staggered halfway through the next day. She tried to look for them, but she couldn't even remember where she had left them. Or where they had left her.

It was as if she had woken from one nightmare into another nightmare. All she had were the clothes on her back and the pad of paper and pencil Ian had given her. Sweet Ian ... where was he? Funny Jory ... was she still making wisecracks? Did Captain Russell ever find his enchanted resort just over the next hill?

Abby sat on the beach, weeping quietly into her hands. Now she had the whole story—or as much of it as she was ever likely to remember. Did the seven survivors on the beach really need to know the awful details?

No! They don't need to know what happened. But I do. I have to find them. I have to know. If they're alive, they must need me, because they needed me before. They're my family.

But Abby realized that she couldn't just tell Daley and Jackson and the others, "Thanks for saving my life and my sanity. Good-bye now." They wouldn't let her go alone back into the jungle, but she couldn't risk their lives, too. Plus, she had to repay them for their generosity and kindness.

More than anything, she had to give them something back for the disruption she had caused in their new lives. These seven people could get along without her. Her family in the wilderness couldn't.

Lex helped his sister and the others to rebuild the fire pit. They laid a new ring of stones and strung up a quick-and-dirty canopy, like the one they had had before. They collected more firewood and cleaned the bottles they had used to put out the fire. But Lex noticed that the usual spirit of teamwork and camaraderie was oddly missing. The fighting and the fire had burned it out of them.

By sunset, everyone was back to doing his or her own thing—Taylor and Eric floating in the brine, Melissa with her candles, Jackson sharpening bamboo stakes, and Nathan and Daley starting a new fire. The mood around the camp was solemn, and most of them ate dinner in small groups.

Lex always had plenty to do, and nothing was more important than scanning for radio signals. He knew it was tedious work, which the others refused to do, but all he needed was to hear one voice amid the static. Then everything would be okay.

As darkness fell upon the island, the teens prepared to go to bed early. They were whipped from the day's insanity, but Lex wasn't tired. The ten-year-old was still working on his radio when Abby suddenly appeared at his workbench. He smiled and waited to hear what she wanted.

Abby peered curiously at him. "Everybody's got something to say about what happened, except you."

Lex shrugged. In his mind, everybody should have said a whole lot less.

"Did I do something wrong?" Abby asked with honest concern.

"I don't think so," Lex answered.

"So much has changed since the crash," she said thoughtfully. "We're all different people."

Lex stopped fiddling with his radio for a moment to really look at Abby. She needed help understanding what was going on, and the bigger kids were all too close to her, or wanted something from her.

"I think it's more like what you said before," Lex answered. "When people go through stuff, it brings them together. We're like a family now, and sometimes families argue."

Abby nodded. "I guess."

"But we look out for each other, too. Like a family. If something bad happens, one of us is right there to help."

The girl mulled over his words and asked, "You'd do anything for your family, wouldn't you?"

He nodded strongly. "Of course. We all would. That's how we made it so far."

Abby granted him a warm smile, and he could understand why all the older boys had lost their brains over her. "You're kinda little to be so smart."

"It's my job," he answered with a shrug. He didn't

add that the older kids were kinda big to be so stupid.

"Would you help me do something?" Abby asked sweetly. There was a glint of mischief in her eyes that made Lex smile and nod his head.

From her hiding place in the trees, Melissa could see Abby and Jackson running to meet each other on the moonlit beach. Their bodies met under the swaying palms, and they held each other tightly. Without saying a word, Abby and Jackson gazed into each other's eyes, and their faces slowly came together. As the waves crashed in the background, their lips met in a passionate kiss.

"No!" Melissa screamed, bolting upright. She stared around at dark canvas, and she heard the waves crashing and faint music in the distance. "Huh?" Melissa said when she realized she was still in her sleeping bag in the girls' tent.

"Is something wrong?" Daley muttered drowsily.

Melissa shook her head and tasted sour jealousy on her lips. "No," she answered. "Just . . . just a nightmare. I need a drink of water."

"Mmmm," Taylor murmured sleepily. "I like that song."

"What song?" Daley asked.

"The one playing on the radio." Taylor rolled over and sat up. "Don't you hear it?"

"Now that you mention it, I do," Daley answered puzzledly. "What's going on?"

All three girls dragged themselves out of their sleeping bags, and Melissa noticed that Abby was not among them. She instantly worried that maybe there was some truth to her dream, and she was the first one out of the tent. Outside, the sound of music was loud enough for everyone to hear.

Daley rubbed her eyes. "What is that? Are the boys doing more night maneuvers?"

"Lex must be awake," answered Melissa. She pointed to the wrecked airplane, which looked all lit up. It even had a pathway of lights leading to it, and the music was definitely coming from the plane.

Melissa heard a male voice grumbling, and she turned to see Jackson crawl out of the boys' tent. A moment later, Eric stepped out, swaying on his feet, then Nathan emerged with his wild hair looking like a bird's nest.

"I was dreaming about music," Eric said drowsily.

"Then we're having the same dream," answered Nathan. He looked over to see the girls. "What's up?"

Melissa pointed to the airplane, and Jackson started heading in that direction. One by one, the others fell in behind their leader. Melissa was delighted to see that the lighted walkway was made from her candles, which looked absolutely beautiful on a tropical beach.

The sky was cooperating with an array of stars that looked like spun sugar spilled on black velvet. Wispy clouds circled the moon, which reflected like a shimmering ball on the dance floor of the vast ocean.

Melissa couldn't believe her eyes. The entire outside of the airplane was decorated with her candles, along with flowers and ferns for table decorations. The airplane seats were arranged on the sand as if guests were expected, and the colorful parachute was suspended over the seats, making it look like an outdoor patio at a fancy restaurant.

Standing in the middle of it was their hostess, Abby, looking gorgeous in a colorful sundress with a white orchid in her hair. Lex was stationed at the mp3 player, deejaying the cool island beat. It was so wonderful and unexpected that Melissa wanted to applaud, and she found herself beaming along with Daley and Nathan. All of them were speechless.

The only one who wasn't speechless was Taylor. "Is that my dress?" she shouted. With fire in her eyes, the blonde started toward Abby, but Eric and Jackson held her back.

After a moment, even Taylor chilled out. This party had taken a lot of work, and anyone could appreciate that. Melissa didn't see any reason why they couldn't have a slice of home on this otherworldly paradise. What a terrific gift from Abby and Lex!

Abby smiled and stepped forward. "You guys have done so amazingly well since the crash," she explained. "I wanted to say how sorry I am for anything I did to mess things up."

Melissa gulped and felt horrible. All the others looked embarrassed, too. Abby had almost died twice and gotten lost twice—it was hardly her fault if she just wanted to live and be happy.

"You haven't messed things up, Abby," Daley answered.

"If anybody's to blame, it's us," Nathan said.

Melissa nodded. "It's true. We've all been immature."

"Yeah, guilty," Eric said, holding up his hand.

Jackson also nodded and held up his hand. Everyone looked at Taylor, who was still pouting over Abby wearing her sundress.

"Fine!" Taylor said, giving in. "What's mine is yours, Abby. Really."

"Thank you," Abby said sincerely. "I said before how bad experiences bring people closer together. I think good experiences do, too. That's why Lex helped me set this up. I wanted us all to share a fun time together . . . and make some happy memories."

Lex put on a popular slow song, and the teens looked uncomfortably at one another. "It's a dance," Nathan said. "Let's dance." He walked up to Abby and held out his hand.

She smiled as she accepted his invitation, and the two of them began to whirl skillfully in the sand. Melissa tried not to look at Jackson, who was standing right beside her, because she didn't want to put any pressure on him. She had already acted enough like a jerk. Besides, he had been curiously flat-footed while Nathan snagged Abby for the first dance.

Melissa didn't look at Jackson, but she couldn't help smiling. This was fun. A dance! Just like that past life, which had seemed to vanish when their plane dropped from the sky. In darker moments, she sometimes wondered if they were ghosts. Maybe they had really died in the crash and were haunting this island, only none of them knew it.

It took a surprise like this to bring her back to life. Tonight, she didn't feel like a ghost.

Finally, Jackson stepped in front of Melissa and said, "I'm not good at this, but—"

Eagerly, Melissa grabbed his hands. "I'll teach you." They danced awkwardly at first, but Jackson was a quick learner. Melissa didn't mind if he jumped all over her feet, as long as his strong arms kept holding her tight.

Eric smiled and extended his hands to both Daley and Taylor. "Well, well, well. Who's the lucky winner?"

The girls laughed and looked at each other. "I think we'll have to get back to you on that," Daley said. Still laughing, the girls began to dance with each other.

"Ouch!" Eric exclaimed. "Don't leave me hangin'!"

On the next song, Abby excused herself from Nathan. "Thank you," she said. Then she walked over to Lex and held out her hand.

The deejay looked horrified. "I don't dance."

"You do now," Abby said with a smile that would not be denied. Lex bravely stood up from his post and began to dance with the older woman.

Melissa was having so much fun watching all of this that she forgot to watch Jackson, and he stepped on her toe. "I'm sorry," he said.

"Me too," she answered sincerely. Jackson held her tighter, and she snuggled against his chest.

Without a partner, Nathan approached Daley and Taylor and asked very formally, "May I?"

Taylor nodded formally. "You may!"

She obviously thought that Nathan was going to ask her to dance, but instead he held out his hand to Daley. The redhead looked very happy to take it, and they instantly fell into each other's arms.

This left Taylor in a royal snit, until Eric moved closer to her. By now, he was almost begging, and Taylor laughed and took his hand.

Four girls and four boys made for a lovely dance under the stars on a tropical island. Eight wasn't such an awful number after all. Melissa glanced around at the other couples. Was it her imagination, or did Daley and Nathan look as if they really enjoyed being in each other's arms?

What did it matter? This was a magical night after an awful day and a pretty bad week, and peace had returned to their makeshift paradise. When the song ended, Lex put on another romantic tune, and the island crew kept swaying under the palm trees.

Nobody noticed when Abby silently slipped away.

NINETEEN

After such a long night, Nathan was surprised that he woke up so early. The golden-red sun was just peeking over the fuselage of the wrecked plane. The DeHavilland no longer looked much like a nightclub, but the flowers and parachute still brightened it up.

Nathan nearly stumbled over an airplane seat that wasn't usually in front of his tent. In the seat was Abby's brightly colored notebook, with her coral-silver necklace draped over an open page. He instantly felt a pang in his gut. This wasn't good.

"Hey! Hey!" he called urgently. Nathan ran around, shaking the tents. "Everybody! Get up ... now!"

Eric stumbled out and looked drowsily at him.

"Is it time for breakfast already?"

"Girls! You too!" shouted Nathan, shaking their tent.

Daley stepped out, followed by Taylor. "Is it time for breakfast already?" Taylor asked with a yawn.

Nathan went back to the airplane seat and grabbed Abby's notebook and necklace, and he scanned the sleepy crowd. Only one of them was missing. "Where's Abby?" he asked.

"She's sleeping," answered Daley with a shrug.

"No, she's not there," Melissa said. "I was the last one out."

Taylor ran back to the tent to check, but Nathan knew she was gone. He began to read aloud the last entry in Abby's notebook. "Please forgive me. This is something I have to do. Jackson, I believe you. It's about right here, right now ... and right now I've got to find the others."

"Hey!" Taylor shouted. "My backpack is gone!"

The others looked stricken with a mixture of shock and guilt and every other emotion. "She must have geared up," Daley said.

Eric slapped his hat on his leg. "When did she do that?"

"Probably last night while we were all dancing," Daley answered.

"There's more," Nathan said. He continued reading. "Please don't follow me, I'll be fine. I know you'll understand because you'd do the same if one of you were lost. I'm going to find them and I'm going to bring them back, I promise. Try not to worry. Make more happy memories. Love, Abby."

Jackson slammed a fist into his palm with frustration. Nathan blurted, "We gotta go after her."

"No. We don't," Jackson answered thoughtfully.

"But what if she gets lost again?"

"Nathan, what are we gonna do?" asked Jackson. "Force her to come back? She'll just go off again."

"Then maybe we can help her find the others," Melissa said.

"And maybe get lost ourselves," Eric added worriedly.

Taylor flapped her arms. "So what do we do?"

That question stumped everyone for several seconds, until little Lex spoke up. "I think we should let Abby take care of her family. She knows the island now. She'll come back."

Daley gave her brother a half-smile. "Hopefully, they'll all come back."

That didn't help ease the pain of losing one of their crew again. Abby wasn't dead, but missing wasn't good, either. Nathan wondered if they could have been more help to her, more understanding. Abby had helped them so much. They were sleepwalking until she got there, and now they felt alive again. Until she returned, they would always wonder . . . and worry.

In a hoarse voice, Jackson said, "Good luck, Abby."

For once, Nathan grabbed a pen and turned to Abby's notebook in order to vent his feelings. That seemed more fitting than the video diary. He wrote:

Abby, you were safe with us, but we know you were never really with us. Some important part of you is still out there with Ian, Jory, and Captain Russell. We understand. You had to go find them.

All of us have felt that way at one time or another. Every time I walk into the jungle to pick fruit, I think about going forward, not turning back to camp. I want to know what's in those mountains, those deep misty canyons, and beyond the blue horizon. I'd also like to find a nice hotel with a shower, a cheeseburger, and a soda.

But I also know there's strength in numbers. No, we're not perfect, and some of us embarrassed ourselves while you were here. But every one of us has done something to support each other on this island. The way Eric spotted your note, the way Taylor found Melissa when she fell off a cliff. You never know which one of us is going to be the hero.

That's why we have to stick together. Love, Nathan.